DIPIKA MUKHERJEE

Mukherjee's debut novel was longlisted for the Man Asian Literary Prize then published as *Thunder Demons* (Gyaana, 2011, South Asia), followed by *Ode to Broken Things* (Repeater, 2016). She has written a short story collection, *Rules of Desire* (Fixi, 2015), and she has edited three anthologies on Southeast Asian fiction: *Champion Fellas* (Word Works, 2016), *Silverfish New Writing* 6 (Silverfish, 2006) and *The Merlion and Hibiscus* (Penguin, 2002).

She won the 2014 Gayatri GaMarsh Memorial Award for Literary Excellence (USA) and in 2009, the Platform Flash Fiction competition (India).

She is Contributing Editor of *Jaggery* and curates an Asian/American Reading Series for the Guild Literary Complex, Chicago.

She holds a doctorate in English (Sociolinguistics), has taught language and linguistics in several countries and is now at the Buffett Institute for Global Studies at Northwestern University.

First published in the UK in 2016 by Aurora Metro Books.

67 Grove Avenue, Twickenham, TW1 4HX.

www.aurorametro.com   info@aurorametro.com

Editor: Cheryl Robson

Aurora Metro Books would like to thank Neil Gregory, Sumedha Mane, Matthew Rhys-Daniel and Ivett Saliba.

10 9 8 7 6 5 4 3 2 1

Printed in the UK by CPI Group (UK) Ltd, Croydon, CR0 4YY.

ISBN: 978-1-910798-39-3 (print)

ISBN: 978-1-911501-12-1 (ebook)

DIPIKA MUKHERJEE

Shambala Junction

Acknowledgements:

A whole world of readers midwifed this book. I couldn't have finished it without my earliest readers: Jan Michaels, Meena Rishi and the wonderful people in my Amsterdam Fiction critique group (Maria Minaya, David Lee, Laura Martz, Ute Klehe, Tim Rease, Dina Nayeri) and the Shanghai Scribblers (Tan Zheng, Kong Peoy Leng, Trista Baldwin, Paul Kurowski, Susie Gordon, Lenora Chu, Jacqueline van der Puye, Francis Yap). My gratitude also to my critique group in Chicago: (Patricia Grace King, Paulette Livers, Rebecca Keller, Mary Anne Mohanraj, Karri Offstein Rosenthal, Angela Pneuman) as well as Dr Serena Wadhwa for some psychological insights. In India, Divya Dubey and Mita Kapur's team gave me invaluable feedback, as did Alpona Dey in the Netherlands.

My gratitude to Nicola Barr who believed in this book before it was fully written, even as I struggled to make sense of it. A Sangam residency at Nrityagram, Bangalore, allowed this book to feel finished. Anjali Singh gave it much-needed direction.

Gratitude always to Prasanta Dutt, Arohan Dutt & Arush Dutt… the anchors in my life, who force me out of the worlds of my creation into a world that is infinitely more amazing. Without you guys this book may have been finished earlier, but my life would be diminished.

The '*Sab Loke Koye…*' poem is adapted from Lalon Fakirs Songs, translated by Azfar Hussain. The poem 'So free am I, so gloriously free' is from Women Writing in *India: 600 BC to the Present*, edited by Tharu and Lalitha. Mutta, who lived 2600 years ago wrote the original poem, and the translation is by Uma Chakravarti and Kumkum Roy.

The details on Indian adoption have been taken from:

E.J. Graff's 2008 article 'The Lie We Love'; David M. Smolin's 2005 article 'The Two Faces of Intercountry Adoption: The Significance of the Indian Adoption Scandals'; and Gita Ramaswamy's 2003 article 'The Baby Harvest: Scandal Over Westerners "Shopping" For Children In India'.

DIPIKA MUKHERJEE

Shambala Junction

AURORA METRO BOOKS

Chapter 1

Iris Sen was used to getting what she wanted. And she wanted this journey. Danesh, her fiancé, had tried to talk her into taking one of the fancy internal airlines to Delhi, but she had been adamant, seduced by the childhood stories about her father's train journeys as a medical student through the hinterlands of India. Flying around India was not enough for this American daughter returning to a homeland after ten years; she insisted on a train, not like the Orient Express but something more, *like, you know, real?*

"What's the point of being in India if we only see the inside of a plane?" she complained to Dan.

"You will not *enjoy* an Indian train."

"I want to see the real India. Meet some real people."

"You'll have plenty of that. Sweaty, dirty, smelly people, surrounding you for hours. Not fun."

"I'm tougher than you think I am, Dan."

7

"You've never been on a bus in your life and you want to do a long-distance train?"

What she didn't say was that Snapchat this past week had been filled with pictures of that emo Rachel LePage backpacking through Europe, knocking at unfamiliar doors that said *Zimmer Frei!* to spend the night... all that adventure on a Eurail pass. How much more awesome, more photogenic, would an Indian train ride be?

She had grown up with stories of camaraderie on an overnight train, and imagined selfies with fellow-travellers, the homemade food in gleaming tiffin carriers and fizzy drinks at every stop. She saw herself slightly dishevelled, grubby but photogenic in a setting more colourful than Europe and seething with life.

"Come on Dan," she cajoled, "if we wanted safe we should have stayed in Ohio! Don't be such a wuss!"

So Danesh caved in (as he usually did), lured by the novelty and Iris' enthusiasm. It was going to be a 24-hour train ride from Kolkata to Delhi, 26 tops, if the train was delayed. How bad could it get?

Iris woke up at 2:35 in the morning to the train shuddering to a stop, then (as she understood very little Hindi and spoke the language not at all), a foghorn of sound. The train compartment was still dimly lit, the sagging curtains partially drawn around the compartment designed for six sleeping passengers. Less than twelve hours had passed since they had boarded this train in Kolkata, but this journey felt much longer. She wasn't ready to admit that she was regretting not taking the plane.

A young man sauntered by, lit by the faint neon light in the corridor, and tossed a paper packet on her feet. Iris had reached out gingerly to read the message smeared in blue ink on the dirty paper: *I only saw your feet... they are very beautiful. Don't let them touch the ground or they will get soiled.*

Chee! Iris sat up. The packet had once held something mildly oily, and she held up the scrawl with her fingertips and wrinkled her nose; God only knows what germs were in the writer's drool. She hurriedly dropped the packet.

This trip to India felt like being thrown into the back of a garbage truck – every surface was coated with something unclean – even the disinfecting wipes here felt contaminated. She had never enjoyed trekking in the great outdoors of America because of the bugs, and here she was, on a train in India, where no place was safe from disgusting diseases and scampering cockroaches. None of the Indian stories she had heard in Ohio had prepared her for this reality; clearly, the community had collectively misimagined their nostalgia for mother India. Her own memories (from a trip to India at the age of twelve) had the unreal quality of old sepia photographs.

By the faded lettering on the sign she could make out they had stopped at Shambala Junction. Peering at her watch again she saw it was 2:39 in the morning and she craned her neck to see Danesh sleeping, his head angled to the front of the topmost sleeper so that their valuables (his backpack, her purse) could be wedged behind his 6 ft 2 frame, far away from casually thieving fingers.

Through the windows of the sleeper compartment, she could see a group of Japanese tourists disembarking. The Indian guide was very solicitous with the geriatric tourists while gesturing imperiously at the coolies flocked around this large group. A young Japanese woman stood slightly apart from the group, finishing an entire bottle of mineral water in one long gulp.

Iris felt thirst tightening the length of her throat. She reached for her bottle of mineral water in the dark and shook it to confirm it was empty; she had finished it before she fell asleep. She could see the man selling tall Bisleri mineral water bottles not too far away on the platform.

Next to the water vendor was a doll-seller, his upper body covered in a threadbare singlet with two dark semicircles around the armpits. He had an array of colourful wooden dolls spread out in front of him on a pushcart: there were dolls with turbans and flared coats playing flutes and *dholaks*; there were men riding horses with colourful stirrups and dazzling sword-sheaths; there were dancers dancing with the left leg slightly on tiptoe, caught in mid-swirl in the disarray of flouncing skirts.

Iris was enchanted. She had once owned a dancing doll just like that one, a beloved painted wooden thing with a crack in the veiled head, a gift from some unremembered relative in her childhood. She wanted some water as much as she wanted to hop off and buy a doll – it would be so cool to find the unblemished twin of the one in her closet in Ohio.

The air outside was refreshingly cool; the doors on both sides of the carriage were open. Immediately, the smell of hot *puris* fluffing into golden balls assaulted her nose. Even at this time of night the *puri* wallah on the platform had a small line of buyers, and he deftly spooned a liquidy potato curry into a leaf bowl as his helper covered it with two piping hot *puris*. The waiting buyer grasped the package and juggled it nimbly as the heat scorched his hands. The train conductor was filling up a red water bottle from a tap. The Japanese tourists were finally moving, after loading all their suitcases and backpacks into a two-wheeled luggage-barrow propelled by four lean coolies.

The train felt solidly still as Iris walked towards the bottles of water. For all she knew, they could be here for another half an hour. The journey so far had been erratic, with stops and starts in the most unlikely places. She looked back nervously at the large Victorian station clock which pointed to 2:41, but the train was totally immobile, as if it too were asleep. As she headed for the drinks stall, she checked for the money pouch attached to her belt and took out a single frayed note.

The cool water trickled deliciously down her throat. She had gulped the entire contents down and was tossing the bottle into a bin when "*Chai garam*," a nasal voice sounded near her waist and a hand simultaneously thrust a small bowl of hot tea in her direction. The tea splashed on her hand and made it feel instantly gummy. She suppressed the instinct to reach for her disinfecting wipes and scrabbled in her money-belt for some change, unwilling to deny the little boy with the dirty towel around his neck his due even though she disliked milky *chai*. The boy took the money as he stared at her, eyes assessing her clothes, breasts and hair, then someone shouted "*Chaiwallah!*" and he turned swiftly, the aluminium kettle in his hand dribbling a line of tea on the platform towards his new customer.

Tea in hand, Iris wandered towards the doll-seller, hesitantly looking back again after a few steps. She walked a little further, sipping the hot tea slowly, blowing her breath into the little opening. As she gulped down the last dregs of liquid, she saw the boy pocketing change from another customer further down and she ran after him along the long platform, to return the little clay bowl.

"Here," she said. "Thank you. Good *chai. Ach-cha.*"

The boy looked at her breasts, outlined through her tight T-shirt, and grinned, ignoring the extended bowl. "Here," Iris tried again. "Your cup."

The boy looked puzzled then, seeing what was in her hand, took her cup, lingering on her fingers a little longer than was necessary, and smashed it against the railway tracks.

"What the…?" Iris looked at the shattered shards in dismay. "Why did you…?"

Then she noticed that many such little clay bowls lay broken along the rails. Eco-friendly, she realised, terracotta to mud, and wondered how to ask the *chaiwallah* for a souvenir cup to show off back home in Ohio.

She followed the boy, who had walked further down the platform and was pouring fresh tea into his aluminium teapot from a frothing saucepan. Two men lounging by a pillar chortled "Hello Dear! Hello Darling!" in her direction, but she walked resolutely on, and tapped the tea boy's shoulder gently.

That was when she sensed a slight rumble, and, heard the deep sigh of air expelled from a lumbering engine. As she whirled around, she could see the train starting to move away. She saw the other tea drinker dash his half-drunk cup against the rails and another one further up the line do the same, and they both swiftly hopped on to the train. Surely the whistle should have blown or something?

Iris' feet remained glued to the concrete of the filthy platform as panic coursed through her blood. The tea-boy poked her waist sharply.

"*Bhago!*" he urged, waving both his hands towards the train as if shooing her there.

Her feet started to move but although she began to jog along the platform she just couldn't run fast enough.

She slid on something slimy and careered into the group of Japanese tourists who stood blocking her dash for the train. Her ankle exploded in pain.

"*Bhago!*" the tea-boy shouted, keeping pace with her, a lot more urgently this time, and his words were echoed by the people around her, all gesticulating for her to move more quickly and shouting encouragement in Hindi. As she continued to run along the platform, the pain in her ankle grew more acute, her chest was exploding and tears began to blur her vision of the departing train.

She didn't see the raised edge of the luggage trolley. Instead, her right toe stubbed on something hard and then it was a blur as she fell into the doll-seller's stand her leg flailing in the air while her hands reached for the ground. There was a crash as the array of wooden dolls tumbled to the ground and smashed.

Iris raised her head very, very slowly to survey the damage. There were beheaded dolls and limbless animals everywhere. The doll-seller was shouting obscenities she barely understood.

Iris felt herself trembling. Anyone could see that she hadn't deliberately destroyed the man's stand. A couple of bystanders kicked at the mangled toy-limbs, while other vendors surrounded the doll-seller, sympathising with one of their own.

She closed her eyes to blot out the sight and the sound and the smells, but it didn't help. It was all too awful. And where was Danesh when she needed him?

Chapter 2

Aman the doll-seller slapped his forehead to smudge the lines of fate. He had been having a terrible day and now it had got even worse with this calamity at the station. The gods were clearly intent on punishing him.

*

His morning had begun at Dr Chipalkatti's Free Maternity Clinic on Mall Road; when Dr Chipalkatti brushed against him but didn't speak on the way out of the delivery room, Aman knew it was a girl. It was the birth of a third daughter.

He had turned 60 two months ago. He finally felt old age press down on his shoulders; a lifetime of his seed, all gone to waste. Every morning, his days started with the unbearable sight of men with sons: *other* men with strong strapping sons who walked tall; sons who brought fat dowries and fatter grandsons into the house and enriched their family in every way.

While he, Aman, could sprout only daughters.

For the last eight months he had been filled with the unspeakable hope that his fortunes now teetered on the brink of change but fate had, with clear malice, dealt him another daughter.

Second wife, third daughter, zero sons. The first wife had been barren and slutty, this second wife might as well have been barren too.

His two daughters, Laila and Shiela, shrank into their grandmother's sari as he strode towards them. Lilavati, their grandmother, squeezed them closer. Lilavati claimed to belong to an aristocratic family of Bengal who had fallen on hard times after the Partition, but who could be sure? Two marriages in a row to a Pathan and a Christian had released her from any caste or religious marks. Now, in her second widowhood, she still retained a certain imperiousness of high birth and she made it clear that Aman was her daughter's mistake, an adolescent error committed by a blooming *jawani* in the hothouse of poverty. She barely even glanced at Aman as she trailed a presence down the corridors of Dr Chipalkatti's clinic, pacing away the time until she was allowed to see her daughter.

Aman shouted at the nurse, who appeared to announce that the baby was now ready to be seen. "See what? Another mouth to feed, another liability to marry off? *Hai Bhagwan*, strange are your ways!"

Lilavati turned on him. "If you must curse anyone at all, curse your own lack of talent! Thirty years of playing your silly *pa-pu* trumpet in wedding bands! And calling yourself an artist! Selling dolls for a few rupees, hah? Look at you, you eunuch of a man!"

And Lilavati clapped her hands, arching them apart, just as the roadside eunuchs did when they danced. It was a most inauspicious start, and the nurse, probably well-used to lamenting relatives at the birth of one daughter let alone the third, left them both alone.

His wife Roop was lying exhausted in a collapsible bed, cradling the baby in the crook of her arm. She had no strength to step between her feuding mother and husband. When Aman reached out to take the baby from her, she surrendered the baby easily, glad to have two arms free to hug her two other daughters.

"Where are you going?" Lilavati asked.

"God be praised, to show the world my beautiful daughter, of course," said Aman, storming out of the room.

Lilavati followed him into the corridor but Aman quickly turned the corner and went down the staircase. All he could see when he looked up again was her indistinct shadow merging into the grimy wall.

Aman walked along the dusty road past the clinic, past the rows of shops that advertised medicine under large green crosses. Saris fluttered in happy colours next to a makeshift stall selling samosas and tea. He turned into the narrow lane where a noisy Parsi troupe had gathered to practise a play, and passed the little primary school which his two daughters attended. A little further, then he stood in front of a Hindi sign that said '*Anath Aashray*'. He could not read the English sign that declared that it was *The*

Sanctuary of Orphans, but his daughter Laila had sounded out the words to show off her English just last week.

As the gates were open and the guard room empty, Aman walked right through.

He hadn't expected this to be so easy and he walked slowly towards the large doors, expecting to be stopped anytime. When there was no resistance, he convinced himself that this was the child's destiny. Everyone was born with a destiny inscribed into their forehead, weren't they? The baby would have a better life if she were adopted by a well-off family. He was actually doing the child a favour.

He placed the baby gently in the wooden crib under the porch. She started to wail immediately and he knew it wouldn't be long before someone heard her and took her in. It wasn't as if he was leaving her in a vat of milk to drink until she drowned. He was simply shaking off his burden and returning her fate to the trusteeship of God.

Aman wandered around aimlessly for hours, unwilling to go home or talk to another person. He didn't know he was heading for anything in particular until he reached the Pathar Ki Masjid and rested. The ancient crumbling stone mosque with the beautiful arched gateway stood framed by the bank of the Ganges.

But there were babies everywhere. Wherever he looked, they were all Aman could see: baby girls bobbing in the murky water; one being carried by a young couple who passed her around like a gift; a baby in the arms of an ayah while the family ate runny ice cream, taking turns to lick from each other's cones with greedy red tongues.

Aman had never seen so many babies, infants swaddled in yellow and white or swamped in pink frills, some with black marks on their forehead to keep away the evil eye.

At the cigarette-seller, as he was lighting his *bidi* from the thick smouldering rope that hung from the awning, he was lightly nudged by a small fist. He wheeled around to see a baby being carried past, the mother's shoulder thick with the toddler's cascading black curls. The child had a thumb in her mouth but with her other hand she had reached for Aman, gently brushing his conscience.

Suddenly, Aman felt remorse overwhelm him as surely as his anger had driven him out of the hospital earlier. He would have to get his baby back. He turned his back on the sacred river and headed for the orphanage without realising that he needed a plan.

*

It was not, Aman argued with himself, as if he could not provide for his family. It was true that he was getting old (turning 60 had been hard), and the jobs were getting more difficult to come by and he was forced to work the night shift selling dolls at the train station. But he was a talented musician and with the heavy demand for wedding bands during the wedding season, the fat bridegrooms and their families still paid him well. Even if that job was seasonal, he could always sell his wooden dolls. It was good that Roop brought in money too by embroidering saris with delicate flowers and sequined trellises, and Lilavati put a roof over their heads through the teaching she did at the school established by Buddhist nuns. But as long as he was in demand as a musician and a doll maker, his family would never starve. Maybe they could even afford three small dowries if the girls grew up to be beautiful.

After all, his mother had been a Bollywood legend of Hindi Cinema and, even after her death, still reigned as the Tragedy Queen. She had been the heroine of the movie of all movies…so what if he was her illegitimate son brought up by a foster family? Her blood still flowed in his veins. His father may even have been a famous actor too – perhaps the great Head-Nodder-Heart-Breaker of the 1950's?

In the days when his looks had been more hero-like, Aman had spent some time in Bombay at the famous movie studios, trying to get the attention of the Sippys and the Kapoors. He had played a few bit parts, but he was mostly an extra, sometimes he was even edited out of crowd scenes. In the front rows of darkened movie halls he would grab Roop, *here, look now, on the left behind the dog*, but even then Roop wouldn't find him quickly enough and he would gladly pay for another ticket just so that she could see him and be proud. Those were good times, then the film offers had started to completely dry up so Aman had found himself on a train to Shambala with Roop, to live with her mother. It was enough that they loved each other and God had given them healthy children — even though they were only girls.

*

The last of the sun's rays were filtering through the lower branches of the huge banyan tree in the courtyard when Aman reached the gates of the orphanage. He was stopped by the guard, who was about to lock the heavy iron gates.

"I need to go inside," said Aman.

The security guard, also from the ranks of the poor, knew at once that Aman was not a potential parent. Obviously a destitute man and a desperate one, he could be treated with abuse. "Go, go," the guard shouted, "Can't you see I'm busy locking up? Come back tomorrow if you have some work…"

"Please, *Saab*." Aman knew that grovelling worked the best in such situations, "May the Gods shower good fortune on you and yours…"

The guard sneered, but Aman did not look away. The guard straightened his shoulders, then, as he raised a hand to shove Aman out of his way, Aman ducked under his armpit and ran through the open gates. He ignored the enraged shouts and ran under the porch and pushed desperately at the heavy wooden doors. They opened, and miraculously, Aman was inside.

A woman sat behind the desk in the dark room, facing the window. Her two forefingers propped up the glasses on her nose as if she were holding her breath. Aman could see her profile clearly, the thick beak-like nose and the wrinkled skin on her neck that hung down to the line of her high-collared black blouse. He tried to speak, but only a squeak came out of his throat.

The woman whirled around, startled. She frowned. "Who are you? How did you get in? Who *are* you?" she asked rapidly.

Before Aman could answer, the guard burst in.

"I left a small baby here earlier today, Madam," said Aman quickly. "A newborn girl."

The woman smiled slightly and waved the indignant guard away. She leaned towards Aman.

"And why did you do that?"

Aman clasped his fingers together and muttered, "I wasn't thinking, Madam… I am not educated, I am stupid, I cannot think. It was wrong. I want to take her back."

The woman still had the half-smile on her face as she appraised Aman's clothes, lingering on the stains on his once-white baggy trousers. She pushed against the floor with the tip of a foot, setting the chair swinging back and forth, back and forth, gently.

"But we did not receive any newborn baby girls today."

There was a buzzing in his ears as Aman stared at her. From the recesses of the house he thought he could hear his daughter crying, but it may have been many babies crying at once or none at all.

"She had a little pink tag… from Dr Chipalkatti's Free Clinic, on her left hand… I left her in the basket…"

The woman's smile vanished. "What you did is a criminal offence. You should have rung the bell and we would have noted the details so that she would be safe. Who knows what happened to her, or even if you left her here at all? There are stray dogs so wild they don't know the difference between a chicken leg and a newborn baby. Anyone could have picked her up…"

Aman hung his head. "She was crying... I thought someone from the orphanage would hear and open the door."

The woman started shouting, "I have no time for this! Maybe the baby was picked up by someone else who was passing and heard her cry? How would I know? What does all this have to do with me?"

She picked up a pencil and twirled it between her fingers. "How do I know that you aren't here to create trouble for us with a non-existent baby? Where is your proof that you left her? We have procedures and rules, you know, we don't buy and sell babies like ripe mangoes in the bazaar! We can't entertain every beggar who claims he has a missing baby!"

She pounded on a flat bell on her desk which resounded with a loud *ping pingg*.

"But– you must have her. Please, Madam..."

The guard reappeared and dragged Aman away. Aman was still shouting when the heavy wooden doors slammed shut. With a kick, the guard sent Aman hurtling into the shrubs outside, where he lay for a while, utterly winded.

His mind raced with thoughts as he lay on the ground. Why wouldn't they give his baby back? He had made an honest mistake! Then he thought about how fragile the baby had looked; why hadn't he noticed then how fair she was, how creamy her skin felt? She had dark locks of hair. She was a beautiful child and he could now see, clearly, that the orphanage Madam would sell her to a brothel. Such fairness, such delicacy of features, would be highly prized. His stomach heaved. If he went to the police, they would probably beat him up, then lock him up for days and his family would never know. Abandoning a baby might be a crime, like that woman had said. Who'd believe his word against hers? After all, what proof did he have?

It was already eight in the evening, the orphanage was closed... there was nothing he could do now, especially alone. So Aman retreated to his usual spot in the railway station where he sold dolls through the evening and night. Here, surrounded by his colourful merchandise, he could think. He rolled out his wheeled cart and unpacked the dolls. First, the slim flute player which he placed next to the two fat men drumming on *dholaks* and finally he positioned the dancer in front, as if she were dancing to their live orchestra. He unwrapped the gods and heroes one after another – Shivaji on his horse, a baby Hanuman playing with a golden sun, Mahatma Gandhi at his spinning wheel – and placed them in their usual spot in his display. His hands moved automatically, with the speed of years of practice, unfaltering, as his mind churned.

One hour passed, then two and four... finally six miserable hours had passed and it was long past midnight as he sat there feverishly thinking up ways to rescue his baby. Trains pulled into the platforms on both sides and departed, without his paying much attention even as the vendors hustled their wares all around him. He had not made a single sale. His mind whirled out plans. Storming the orphanage with some men from his neighbourhood as soon as the gates opened in the morning – could that work? Miracles happened all the time, like last year, when that man left his unwanted daughter to die in the wild, even covering her skin with the sap of a poisonous plant, but that child had been rescued in time and was well, wasn't she? His baby, too, would be back soon. He just had to act quickly.

*

A light rain started to fall and the damp earthy smell wafted into his nostrils. With such a heavy cloud of worry hovering over his head, he didn't notice the train hissing into silence on the platform like hot steel meeting water. The boys with the tea-kettles bustled about and the food-sellers started shouting out their wares. Aman was too despondent to call out to any potential customers and even the little girl who had stared greedily at his bridal pair had been dragged away by her father before she could be wheedled into a purchase. Then the shouting on the platform made him look up to see a young woman jogging after a departing train, her eyes wide, her ample breasts jiggling about beneath her T-shirt as she ran.

He turned his head to gauge just how far away the train was, which is why he didn't see her coming. Instead, he felt the sudden shove of his wheeled trolley and heard the crash before he looked back to see the stupid girl land at his feet with a thud. Two giant suitcases which she'd knocked off a luggage trolley flopped down behind her, crushing his dolls as they lay scattered all around.

Aman's display (or what was left of it) looked like he had set up a tableau of the Kurukshetra battlefield. There were beheaded dolls and limbless animals everywhere.

Chapter 3

The crowd was milling around her, noisy in their concern, as an old woman bent over her to sprinkle some cold water on Iris' face. Iris touched her face gently, extracting shards of wood, expecting to find blood. Looking up, she met the furious eyes of the doll-seller, who was cursing her loudly. She felt strong hands lifting her up into a sitting position and then she stood up to see the train disappearing in the far distance, chugging on, turning a corner until its long tail merged with the inky night.

"You pay! You pay! Eighty thousand rupees! Now! You pay me!" the doll-seller was shrieking, waving irate hands over his display, looking as if he was going to punch her in the face.

Just then, another train pulled in on the other side of the platform. The crowd of passengers around her quickly assembled their belongings and headed for the train. There was a sudden frenzy of activity and all the women who had surrounded her departed, one stroking her arm in a sympathetic good bye. Then the second train was also gone, leaving Iris alone with the motley crew of vendors. A very aggrieved group of men.

Iris grabbed at the small money-belt around her waist. As her hand closed over the small pouch, she remembered with growing horror that her handbag was on the train, wedged behind Danesh's head. She didn't have a mobile phone and she certainly had not memorised Danesh's mobile number – they had bought their Indian SIM cards in Kolkata only five days ago – what was she going to do? She couldn't call her parents either, as they were on a wellness retreat in the Himalayas (no phones, no meat, no alcohol) and would be completely unreachable for another week. She felt faint at the prospect of being completely alone, surrounded by aggressive men demanding money in a language she barely understood. Money that she clearly did not have.

Did Danesh even realize she was missing?

As she turned from the tea-boy to hide her watering eyes, she was confronted by two leering men who jostled each other gently as they looked her up and down and grinned. Iris doubted if there was a single man in this country who wasn't a pathetic lecher.

Aman glared at the girl angrily while the vendors swarmed around, all urging him to do *something*, baying for her blood. He wished they would be quiet. He wanted to think clearly and get his money back. The last thing he needed was for this agitated group of men to become violent. Then there was the sound of a scuffle, a glimpse of a saffron sari, and Maitri, the bookseller, materialised next to the girl.

Aman sighed with relief. Maitri had a Buddhist bookstall at the station, and was Aman's neighbour. Her English was pretty good.

Maitri swivelled her neck to stare down the loafers surrounding the girl. "Does she look like your sister that you are swallowing her with your eyes? Or your daughter, hah, you motherfucking *bhenchods*?" Immediately, the crowd of vendors stepped back. Maitri had been born in a brothel, and her language was coarser than any of them. There was not a single man in Shambala who would take *pangas* with Maitri, especially when she was defending another woman; Maitri headed a group of Buddhist nuns who gathered at the homes of wife-beaters and alcoholics and she was as intrepid as she was caustic.

The foreigner bent down to massage her left ankle and winced in pain. Maitri immediately bent down to examine her foot. The two started a hesitant conversation, which picked up speed with much clucking by Maitri. Aman gulped. If he did not act fast the girl would disappear, into a clinic or hospital maybe, and he would never see her again. He needed Maitri on his side.

Aman started to babble about his broken dolls and his lost income emphasising that he had a growing family to feed, with another daughter born just this morning. While Maitri was distracted, a man edged closer to the girl. As the girl gripped the pouch around her waist and glanced nervously about, Maitri gave the loitering man a hard shove.

"We will have to help the girl find a place to sleep tonight." Maitri said.

"Yes, yes," agreed Aman immediately. "The girl cannot stay here all night."

Maitri looked at him appraisingly. "… You will get your money, but not now. We must help her find her family first. I need to close my store, and then we can go." The girl sat desultorily on the bench, close to tears. A group of vendors smirked in the far corner, making suggestive comments about where she could spend the night if no one took her home

Maitri asked the girl, "You want a hotel? A nice clean place, near railway station, not too much money?"

The girl looked confused. "My purse is on the train. I only have a few hundred rupees." She clearly trusted Maitri although she was still wary of Aman. She turned slightly toward Maitri, took out her money pouch and showed Maitri the notes.

Aman counted the sparse offering with his eyes. Maitri sighed and shook her head. "Not enough. Train ticket tomorrow or hotel tonight… both you cannot do."

The girl shrank further into the bench and covered her face in her hands. "I am so screwed," she whispered. Maitri looked at Aman and said in Hindi, "She has no money to go anywhere else. I will take her home tonight… but after that?"

"Bank," asked Aman desperately, his voice rising again, "ATM? Credit Card?"

The girl sniffled, turning the money pouch and unzipping its lone pocket to show that there was nothing else inside. Aman sat down on the other side of the bench. This stupid girl really had *no* money.

The vendors lost interest and started packing up their wares and wandering away. Even the *puriwallah* was packing away the last of the deflated golden balls on top of his small kerosene stove and gathering his utensils. The coolies were finding dark corners to sleep in. The tea-boy watched them from a distance while tucking all his utensils into a dirty aluminium pail and emptying out his teapot onto the tracks.

He and Maitri would just have to look after the girl until she contacted someone to pay for the damages. He started to sort through his broken dolls, packing away the few that still seemed to be in one piece. He kicked at the broken wheel of his cart, feeling as though his whole world was falling to pieces.

Maitri gestured at her bookstall. "I close my shop now," she told the girl. "You wait, this is Aman, he will stay here with you, don't worry, I will come back and we will go to my house. Don't worry. You are safe here."

The glance she threw over her shoulder as she walked away told Aman to behave himself. The station was starting to look deserted. The girl looked behind her but the Station Master's office was dark.

"Ticket?" The girl pointed at the closed shutters of the ticket booth framed by wide arches.

"Marning." He snarled.

All the girl could think about was getting away on the next train? Aman angrily busied himself trying to straighten the old cart. It sloped at a most unnatural angle and he kneeled down, tinkering with the broken wedges and trying to salvage what he could.

He looked up at the sound of the girl weeping. She was holding a broken doll, the one dressed as a bride, and she cried like a small child, her face and lips dissolving in her tears.

"I am so sorry, so sorry…"

Aman had to sit down on the ground then at the sudden memory of his baby wailing in the background as he walked away from the orphanage. He took a long breath. "*Madamji*," said Aman shakily. "I help you." He pointed to his chest. "Myself Aman. I help. Maitri help. Tomorrow, marning, help…" He felt himself falter as his limited English vocabulary spent itself and he tried to ignore the tears pricking at the back of his eyes.

Chapter 4

Iris didn't think she had much of a choice. The night was growing darker as the station grew more deserted. The shadows already looked more frightening than the old man – his name was Aman? – in front of her. She didn't think that he would be able to overpower her even if he was the lecherous sort. And the woman, Maitri – she spoke English – which was a relief. When the two of them, Aman and Maitri, had spoken to each other, she understood that they were trying to help her. But her Hindi was so limited that she would just have to trust her instincts about them. But then again, it was her instincts that got her off that train in the first place. What if these two had a number of nasty accomplices waiting outside to sell her into a life of sexual slavery? Would she end up like that poor Delhi girl raped and murdered in a bus?

Get a grip, she thought, remembering how Maitri had dealt with the men on the platform. Nothing bad would happen if Maitri was with her. She needed to work on her courage.

"Come. We go home now." Maitri had returned.

Iris' panic rose again as she looked around the station. The fluorescent light above the sign *Internet Café* blinked into darkness, then flickered on again. Every doorway either had a grill or a shutter that was closed. The pain in her ankle was excruciating.

"*Madamji?*" Aman beckoned with an index finger for her to follow, then turned away to walk towards the exit. Iris' thoughts whirled chaotically inside her head. *Why did this man want to help her after she had destroyed his shop? How could she trust these strangers?*

She watched Aman's back walking away from her. Iris took a deep breath, then looked uncertainly at Maitri. Maitri smiled back. They followed Aman out of Shambala railway station, walking past the rows of sleeping bodies huddled into their own clothing, the women with sari ends pulled over their faces and the men with cloth bundles under their heads. Arms were flung over eyes, shuttering them from the lights, and there was the stench of sweating bodies cramped into tiny spaces. Aman headed for a line of auto rickshaws and Iris followed.

She watched silently as he thwacked the front of a vehicle with the palm of his hand then shook the driver vigorously. The auto rickshaw driver had been asleep, but he didn't seem to mind being so violently disturbed. He took the grey towel from under his head and slapped at the seats a couple of times, dislodging stray food particles. Iris found herself with Maitri in the larger back seat, while the auto rickshaw driver and Aman perched on the tiny seat in front. As Maitri's sweat-sour smell assailed her nose, Iris's fingers itched for the disinfecting wipes on the train, now completely unreachable. The horror of her situation hit her again.

Maitri turned to look at her. "Please. Not to worry."

Iris felt too panicked for a coherent response. She was alone with complete strangers in a dark vehicle in an unknown city. Her body tautened, prepared for any eventuality. But as the auto rickshaw made its way through the night streets a strong breeze blew in, forcing her to shield her hair away from her eyes, she started to uncoil in the silence with its mysterious shadows. There was a padded silence to the night, like being suspended between wakefulness and sleep.

Except that she could not really relax. This was all her fault, for stepping off the train so thoughtlessly. Iris frowned: Danesh would wake up and be frantic. Had he contacted her parents already? How long would it take him to realise that she wasn't in the toilet or somewhere else?

An involuntary gasp escaped her lips. Where was the nearest American consulate? The driver and Aman both turned around for a fleeting glance (Maitri seemed to be asleep) then looked away again. Her mind raced on, searching for a solution in this foreign place where she didn't know anyone – hadn't someone once warned her not to get into an auto rickshaw with two men in front? – and she barely knew the language. She imagined herself on a lone dark highway like this one, having to fuck her way back to civilization. A sudden stillness shook her out of her thoughts.

The vehicle had stopped and Aman hopped off. He was giving the driver a single note while Maitri groggily stepped out. Iris clambered out quickly. As the auto rickshaw lights disappeared into the darkness, Maitri gently guided her with a hand on her arm until Iris stood at the mouth of a thin alleyway. Her senses heightened, as she entered such a dark, narrow place. There were whispering sounds and rustles and Iris curled her toes, expecting rats.

"Come, *Madamji*," said Aman. "Come." She followed him past a nauseating drain she could smell well before she saw its viscous bubbling surface in the faint moonlight. Something scurried across her path, startling her, but it was only a small lizard with a long tail. Her ankle felt much better, but one more twist and she would be down in this dark filth.

Iris couldn't see much in the darkness of the alley and she bumped into Aman, who had stopped. He stood immobile in the middle of a three-way intersection and stared straight ahead. Although she could not see his face, she could feel the tension in his rigid back. She followed his eyes. He was looking at the jumbled block of apartments at the end of the lane. On the ground floor of the block closest to where they stood, next to the second door, lay two large bodies with two smaller ones sprawled out.

Then Aman remembered he had the only key to his house. Usually his front door was never locked – someone was always at home – now, in a flash of clarity, he saw himself, hours ago, lifting the key from behind the damp towel and pocketing it. He smacked his forehead. Roop had been at a free charitable clinic. They wouldn't have kept her any longer than absolutely necessary. He had to think fast. He still had no idea where the baby was. As soon as his mother-in-law awoke, she was sure to give him a loud tongue-lashing, and Roop, oh Roop, what could he possibly say to her? He looked nervously at Maitri, who yawned sleepily next to the stupid foreigner. That girl was nothing but trouble. Seeing his family sleeping outside like homeless beggars convinced him that this girl was probably a cursed nemesis whom the Gods had sent to punish him for the sin of abandoning his own baby.

"Wake them up and take them inside, Aman!" hissed Maitri. "I will take the girl home. Why is Roop sleeping with the baby outside like this when she just gave birth this morning?" Aman nodded and stepped closer to his family, hoping that the keen-eyed Maitri wouldn't notice that the baby was not with Roop. But Maitri, filled with some stupid maternal instinct continued to whisper, "The poor baby, sleeping outside her own home!" Maitri paused. "Oye! Where is the baby, Aman?"

"You can see the baby tomorrow," Aman said hurriedly. He put his fingers on his lips and waved his arms to indicate that Maitri and the girl should leave quickly and quietly. But Maitri looked at him mutinously: "Show me you have the key you idiot," she hissed in fury, "leaving your family to sleep outside like this! If you have lost the keys, you son of an imbecilic owl, Roop and the baby can come to my house…" and she continued to grumble about dim-witted men under her breath.

The girl continued looking at both of them, making no comment and doing nothing to hurry Maitri on. The stars were clearly misaligned so that his luck would get worse and worse until he dropped dead, which wouldn't be a bad thing as he wouldn't have to explain anything to Maitri or Roop or his mother-in-law anymore.

As Aman scrabbled around his pocket for the single key, he worried about what he could possibly say to Roop. Perhaps she would understand, she loved him so much... he could barely think as Maitri continued to mutter loudly. But what could he possibly say that would make a difference? As if prodded by his thoughts, Roop stirred and slowly sat up. Aman saw his wife staring at him, then squinting at the young woman by his side. Roop was gaping at both of them in disbelief. A thin sound, like a small gargle, started in her mouth. Woken by that sound, Lilavati, his mother-in-law, jerked up and clutched at her back, cursing at the pain and old age. Then she saw Aman and her curses grew louder and more colourful. This was nothing Aman hadn't heard before, so he strode quickly past the two women and unlocked the door. The two women fell in after him, hurriedly, as if they expected the door to slam shut. Roop clutched at Aman and shook him; she looked like she was crying. Then Lilavati started to hit Aman on the head: smack, smack, smack!

"Where *is* the baby?" asked Maitri in English, but to no one in particular. "Roop had a baby just this morning..." her voice trailed off.

Iris watched the tableau unfolding before her in growing horror. She couldn't believe that the two sleeping bodies at the front door were still asleep in the middle of this ruckus. Then a light went on upstairs and someone began shouting down, while others drifted out of doorways to see what was going on. One young man squatted near her and scratched his balls while staring at her.

Finally, the two sleeping children woke up and ran inside the house with cries of *Ma!* Iris wondered whether Maitri would do something to help the hapless doll-seller before the women drew blood, but Maitri seemed completely lost in her own thoughts.

Meanwhile, the scrotum-scratcher had started to stealthily inch closer to Iris while singing an erotic Bollywood number she actually recognized. Iris touched Maitri's shoulder and the older woman grabbed her hand, leading her towards Aman's house. Maitri slammed the door behind her as they entered the house, shutting out the collective gasp of dismay from the audience watching the domestic drama. The noise of the door slamming also had the happy effect of making the two women already in the house freeze in shock. They glared at Iris and Maitri.

"Where is the baby?" asked Maitri, unperturbed.

"That's what we want to know," shouted the older woman. She pointed a bony finger at Iris, "Maybe you know?"

Iris smiled widely to show off the white teeth that had been polished to perfection before her trip to India. She had no idea what else to do. The older lady looked her up and down in disgust. Then she growled at Iris in Hindi, "Who are you?"

"Amreekan," explained Maitri. "Only English."

Iris looked at Aman, the poor, poor doll-seller. First she had destroyed his dolls, and now this man was clearly in trouble with his family. Over some baby. The man was on the floor, sobbing into his folded arms, and he looked very old and broken too. On the walls there were tattered film posters. One showed a woman with tears of red blood flowing from large eyes. Maitri saw her glancing at them.

"That's Aman's mother... The Queen of Tragedy," explained Maitri quickly.

"A Bollywood star?"

The old woman marched up to Iris and snarled, "What do you want with him?"

Iris took a deep breath and started, "My train...," she said, "I get off," and then with fingers running away, "it go, I fall..."

The old woman seemed to choke on her own spit. "I can speak English," she said belligerently. "I look like a beggar to you, hanh?"

Iris back-pedalled quickly. "I'm sorry," Iris indicated the man on the floor, "he didn't speak much English, so I thought..."

The old woman shoved the doll-seller's shoulder with a pointed toe. "He's a piece of dog shit."

Iris wasn't sure how to respond. The part of her that felt like bursting into giggles at the absurdity of her situation was held back by the fury in the old woman's eyes.

"Tell me how you know my worthless son-in-law," the old woman ordered. Another shove with her vicious toe. "You help him bury his new daughter?"

Iris' eyes widened as Aman cowered. She shook her head slowly while Maitri started to explain what had happened at the railway station.

Over the next hour, Iris found herself warming to Lilavati. Lilavati was telling Maitri about the missing baby (making it clear that it was Aman's *version*), while Maitri

39

commiserated. Then both women sighed and there was a long silence.

"Nothing more you can do tonight," said Maitri. "The orphanage gates will be locked. Better to go with Aman again in the morning. Try to get some rest now."

"How can I rest? That fool! I will go, alone, as soon as the sun rises."

"He will go anyway, so go together, you'll be stronger. Roop needs to rest, look at her, so agitated… I will tell the Buddhist nuns to come in the morning, in case you need our help."

"We must call Lakshmy Mittal…"

"Yes, I thought of that, but Lakshmy's fighting the Chaya case in the Allahabad High Court now. She'll be back in a few days… I'll phone her in the morning." Maitri gave Lilavati's hand an encouraging squeeze, "Maybe you will bring the baby back tomorrow and we won't need anyone's help!"

Lilavati just stared gloomily at Aman and Roop. Maitri turned to Iris to change the topic. "Iris! What kind of name is that? Your mother not Indian?"

Iris was used to such questions by now and explained that her mother had named her Iris, when her friend Mrs Mehra had come bearing *parathas* in a dish decorated with irises, shortly after her birth. Her mother had said, 'I will name her Iris, to remember this perfect moment.'

Lilavati rolled her eyes. Then, reaching out for a betel leaf and spreading a brown goo on it with her finger, she tucked a wad of green leaf into a corner of her mouth and chewed hard. Red spittle formed at the corner of her mouth. "So, where is your husband now?"

"He's – he's on the train. Probably still sleeping."

"Men, hah! Sniff like dogs, sleep like dogs! I hope he comes looking for you once he wakes up."

Iris had never considered the possibility that Danesh wouldn't. She may have had some reservations about marrying Danesh, especially as his mother was such an interfering old witch, but it had never entered her mind that Danesh could have any doubts about her. Iris furrowed her brow and Lilavati laughed, "Men! All pumping cocks and nothing else, let me tell you, maybe your husband lost you on purpose, hahn?"

Maitri said something to Lilavati in rapid Hindi that made them both laugh. Then Lilavati grew serious. "Men lose women all the time," Lilavati told Iris, "See," she pointed at Aman, "he left his baby in an orphanage because he didn't want another *girl*."

Iris stared at Aman and Roop huddled in a corner of the room. They seemed to be rocking back and forth and Roop was howling while beating her chest. Lilavati spat out a red rivulet into a small bowl. It sat beside her like congealing blood. Iris looked away. "Where is the baby now?"

Maitri said, "We will get her back from the orphanage tomorrow."

Iris let the silence grow. She was alone in a foreign city and clearly dependent on the kindness of strangers. If these women thought she was respectably married, it could only help. It was such a relief to be able to speak English that Iris was desperate for the sympathy of these two old ladies. Iris' lips contorted into a yawn. "Train... tomorrow morning?"

"OK, we go to sleep now. I will help you get on a train tomorrow. If your husband isn't here already, that is. You are going to Delhi, yes, lots of trains, all day, all the time. Don't worry. Sleep now."

In Maitri's tiny room next door, Iris immediately tumbled into the charpoy in a corner. She thought about getting up to brush her teeth with her fingers, surely they had toothpaste here? She had never felt so filthy or so exhausted in her entire life. She briefly registered the discomfort of being poked by the sharp ropes of the charpoy, but even before Maitri could put a thin cotton sheet on her, she was fast asleep.

*

After spreading the sheet over her sleeping guest, Maitri lay down on the ground. Through the porous wall she could hear Roop snivelling over Aman's urgent words. She heard him repeating how much he regretted leaving the baby in an orphanage and then not being able to find her again. Maitri hoped that Roop would now come to her senses and kick this worthless idiot out of her life. She liked Aman as a friend, but she wouldn't want a daughter married to him. No wonder Lilavati was so irritable.

Lilavati claimed that she had grown up in an aristocratic Bengali family but the Partition of India had given many people a new slate on which to rewrite a family tree. It was probably true that Lilavati had worked with Mother Teresa's Shishu Bhavan in Kolkata in the early years, for she was good at talking to the broken and the hopeless.

Now Maitri and Lilavati taught basic literacy to the girls growing up in the slums, but Lilavati was tiresome about chastity; if Lilavati had her way, none of their students would ever get married, but take a vow with a religious order like the Buddhist nuns instead. No one took her seriously. And all this because Roop had married that worthless musician, Aman. The apartments they lived in belonged to the Buddhist nuns and Roop would still have a roof over her head if she threw Aman out, but she loved that idiot much too much.

Maitri looked at the sleeping Iris and smiled in the darkness. This girl would be malleable. The thought hatching in her head for the past hour grew in detail – if what Aman had said about the orphanage was true, the girl could help them get the baby back. Aman, on his own, would just get kicked out again. She started to fine-tune a strategy in her head.

Tomorrow, Lilavati would go with Aman and deal with the orphanage. Aman had probably retreated at the first sign of danger, but Lilavati was made of sterner stuff. If they didn't succeed in getting the baby back tomorrow, Maitri had an excellent alternative ready. She and the Buddhist *Bahini*, their army of nuns, together they would bring the child came back home.

43

Chapter 5

Iris felt her muscles spasm as she whirled out of a deep sleep into sudden wakefulness. *My father lost my mother at a fair.* A voice whispered inside her head.

Peering into an unfamiliar darkness, Iris felt a small fist hammering in her heart, *thik-thik-thik-thik, true-true-true-true.* She hadn't heard this tempo except in her nightmares; now she felt trapped within the recurring nightmare she'd had from the time she was seven years old. Usually, she would awake from her nightmare in her own bedroom, but as she looked around in a panic at the small dark room, she realized that tonight she was alone with her fears.

The nightmare was always the same – looking up, she saw vultures circling the barren field where she lay, their long black wings patiently fanning the hot sky. Why was she dreaming about this again? Why tonight? This was a memory she had deliberately erased and Iris hadn't consciously thought of it for over a decade, but now, when she, herself, was lost, this memory felt like a premonition. She curled into herself, letting the rope-stringed bed jab into her side. She heard Maitri snoring somewhere in the darkness and felt even more alone with a complete stranger.

My father lost my mother at a fair. Or she left him, and she left me. Which was it? Thik-thik-thik-thik, true-true-true-true.

She saw her mother's face, from that day in Ohio so long ago, telling her. 'Your father once lost me at a fair. I thought he would never come back. I wasn't sure I wanted him back either.'

It all started with her grandfather dying. Her mother had wanted to go back to India to stay with him until his last rites. There were tearful phone calls and her parents kept arguing.

"I will not come back," her mother had shouted at her father behind the shut bedroom door, but she didn't say these words to Iris.

"Who will look after Iris if you run away like this?"

"Let me take her then, she can go to school in Calcutta!"

"Hah! Then I will see neither one of you again. You think I don't know that? You'd let her die of a disease there before you'd come back to me."

"Yes, yes! There are *so* many ways to die in India, you more than anyone else should know that."

"You will *not* take Iris!"

"How long will she be my chain? How many more years, Dhiman?"

Iris remembered rushing to her father, and clinging to his waist, crying, "I want to go with Ma! Send me now, I don't want to be here!"

As her father sat, stupefied, Ma had shaken Iris with uncharacteristic fury and said, "Behave yourself, Iris, before you get a slap."

Enraged, Iris turned on her mother. "OK! Go back to your own Ma and Daddy! I hate you both! I wish I was dead!"

Then her mother had pulled her aside, and spoke to her in a low, intense tone. While Ma spoke, Daddy sat, sad and frozen, as if isolated behind a pane of glass.

"Whether you are old enough to hear this or not, I am going to tell you something." Ma had taken a jagged, deep breath, "This has nothing to do with you, or how much I love you. My sister was the one your father always wanted to marry. I married your father because she died. This is about your father and me, and nothing to do with you."

"Why can't I go with you, Ma?"

"Because… I need time."

"Ma, please…"

"… Your father and I… we were married to keep our parents happy. One day, I got lost at a fun-fair. I wasn't sure your father would even come back to look for me. But he did… because I was pregnant… with you. That was the only reason."

"So I came to this new country. I longed for the Bengali of my books, of speech, of the gentle repartee of equal and intelligent conversation. You were growing inside me, Iris, and for a while, motherhood was enough. Of course my studies stopped, there was no one to look after you, and I was stupid and speechless in the alphabet of this distant and cold harbour. There was a 24 hour Wal-Mart near the apartment, and when I would wake up in the middle of the night to feed you, I would wander out of the door, walking all night in the aisles of the supercenter, looking for something I couldn't buy in all the excess. I still have that addiction, of needing to walk for hours through empty spaces, speaking to myself, in Bengali, in my own mind."

Daddy reached out to Ma, as if to draw her to him. "Enough," he whispered urgently, "she is only a child!" But Ma ignored him and continued:

"I will be here for you, always. I will come back for you."

Daddy got up abruptly, pushing his chair so savagely it fell with a thud. The sliding door closed behind him as Ma's eyes followed him. Then Ma took another jagged breath, her eyes tearful. "I have to go back home for a while. But I promise I'll come back for you." And Iris had burst into tears, "Will Daddy lose me too while you're gone?"

*

Iris stretched out a foot gingerly over the dark contours of the bed and felt a sheet under her foot. She heard a gentle snore, and looking over, she saw Maitri on the ground. Why was Maitri sleeping on the ground? Nothing made any sense here. She quickly sat up again and hugged her knees, curling into herself.

Her mind was alert. Just like that time when her world shattered when she was seven years old, now her world had turned upside down again. Like her mother, she had gone back to India, to see her relations. Like her mother, she was doing what her family wanted and marrying Danesh. Hadn't they been pushed together ever since she could remember? Her whole childhood, trying to fit in with the kids at school, trying to stay out of the sun so her skin would stay lighter, changing her name to something more readily accepted – all of this had been for what?

Here in this squalid room, none of that mattered. Perhaps it never did? *Thik-thik-thik-thik, truth-truth-truth-truth*.

*

The sharp patter of raindrops on a tin roof brought Iris back into her surroundings. The *thik-thik-thik-thik* nightmares had been intense at one time, waking her up almost every single night until her mother had returned from India. By the time Iris was ten, her father stayed in the house for just long enough for their rages to continue.

They had made a brief trip to India when Iris was twelve. She remembered, very vaguely, the faces of too many relatives in Kolkata, but what she remembered most clearly was the enormous marble bathtub in the hotel in Bombay where they had stayed for five days while her father attended a medical conference while her mother stayed with her grandmother in Kolkata. Iris didn't have any grandmothers alive in Kolkata anymore. This trip with Danesh had been hasty and surreal – they had stayed at the Park Hotel like American tourists, and cousins had met them at Flury's and Shiraz.

The invitations to home-cooked meals were politely declined except for one, where they ate in a small verandah as a baby tore up the pages of a magazine and the acrid smoke of burning twigs wafted up from the street.

Iris found it hard to connect with her Indian cousins, although they were the same age. She felt gauche and childish while being helped into a sari that everyone else wore with such graceful ease. Her attempts at Bengali were met with smiles and bursts of appreciation, as if she were a toddler learning to speak, instead of a grown woman. She had been completely humiliated when she asked for a specific cut of fish in the curry and had mispronounced it as a donkey, and a six-year-old child had laughed so hard that he started to hiccup uncontrollably.

In Ohio, she had navigated the Indian gatherings with ease, knowing just how to riff off the Indian-born aunties and uncles, knowing just enough Bengali food terms and greetings to make the older people smile, before retreating into a huddle with the American-born children who spoke the exact same language and understood all the jokes.

It didn't help that she became Shinjhini again in India. Ma was Nupur Sen, the name on the American passport she carried now, and Nupur (which meant *anklet* in Bengali), had named her Shinjhini, the sound of dancing bells.

Sometime, along the way, at a summer camp, to Ma's despair, she had wilfully become Iris from Shinjhini, constructing an easy fable about her birth and irises on dinnerware. Now the Indian relatives refused to call her Iris. Shinjhini slid musically off their tongues; no one came to the stuttering quizzical stop at 'Shin', like in America.

A burst of lightning lit up the room, falling on a series of movie posters. The stylized Bollywood poster nearest to Iris flared into thick brush lines leaving nothing open to interpretation – and Iris realized with a sense of shock that the heroine on the poster was weeping a thin line of red blood. The embossed red line faded as the lightning changed to a clap of thunder. She cowered under the thin sheet, willing herself to wake up from this. *Thik-thik-thik-thik, truth-truth-truth-truth*, went her heart. She slipped down into the bed until she could pull the sheet over her head. Agitated and almost suffocating in the moist heat, she struggled to fall asleep again.

She remembered Ma's soft hands stroking her hair: "I will always come back to you *Mamoni*. Always… Your father didn't want to lose me – it was an accident, he didn't lose me, and we are both trying very hard. You should know that, no matter what else I have said."

*

Years later, in the face of Iris' doddering performance in school, her mother would laugh sarcastically about the apple falling very far from the tree. When her cohorts from the desi community were applying and getting accepted into Yale and MIT and Princeton, and Iris barely made it to a large state university, her father joked about all the money saved in tuition.

No one, Iris realized with a jolt now, ever expected anything of her. Occasionally, she still woke up to the image of vultures circling an arid field, their patient wings barely stirring the air, and *thik-thik-thik-thik* hammering in her heart. But tonight, nothing would transport her out of the nightmare and into the safety of her own bedroom.

In the darkness of this humid night, it didn't help that she was in this strange room, next to the sleeping body of a stranger, where absolutely nothing was familiar.

Chapter 6

Aman and Roop didn't sleep at all. When Lilavati awoke at dawn, they were both pacing near the door. Aman couldn't wait for the sky to lighten; even Lilavati's curses did not get the usual response as he soothed his wife. He described a triumphant return with the baby in his arms with the orphanage Madam trailing behind him in handcuffs, but Roop was too furious. She was adamant about leaving him today and never coming back unless he brought her baby back to her. In hurried sentences, Aman and Lilavati decided to go to the orphanage while Roop stayed at home. Roop was still weak and bleeding from the birth; Lilavati had to tell her, quite harshly, what a liability she would be if she insisted on trailing along.

Lilavati and Aman boarded a sputtering bus in the morning rush hour and arrived at the orphanage by nine in the morning, which was when it opened to the public. Unable to spew too much venom at her son-in-law in public, Lilavati settled for glaring at Aman with barely contained hostility throughout the journey.

Aman was recognised at once. As he and Lilavati made their way to the gates of the orphanage, the senior guard took the precaution of holding up his stick and slicing it through the air in a practice swing. A junior guard stood up immediately and they blocked the small opening with their bodies. Although the older security guard kept an unwavering eye on them as they approached, the assistant guard, a young teenager who wavered between boredom and menace, was quite distracted by a passing young woman whose fire-engine-red veil fluttered in the breeze.

"What do you want now?" the older guard growled. Aman opened his mouth, but only a high squeak came out as the older guard's stick sliced through the air again. Lilavati straightened her back, and in her slow formal English, enunciated, "We want to see Madam. Have appointment."

The senior guard momentarily paused, then his eyes took in Lilavati's cheap *tangail* sari, which, although her best, had fraying threads of gold clearly visible at the paisley bordered edges. He looked Aman up and down again, nudged his accomplice with an elbow and hollered, "*Heb pointmen, Memsaab?*" in a parody of her English. Then the two guards roared with laughter while instructing Aman and Lilavati, in very rude Hindi, to get lost. Lilavati bristled. She shouted, in Hindi this time, that they obviously did not have any mothers or sisters or daughters at home, otherwise they would at least have some manners. She plonked herself down on the ground, right by the gate, and said she was going to stay there until someone let her see the Madam.

Even the older guard's uncouthness had its limits – he couldn't bring himself to physically remove a woman, especially not one old enough to be his mother. He looked at her wizened face and spat on the ground, giving himself time to think.

The younger guard scowled at Aman while chewing on a blade of grass. "Shall I wallop this bugger now, or do you want to do it yourself?"

Aman's head spun. He wanted to demand to see his baby but wondered whether some grovelling would work better than anger. In the background, he could hear the familiar sound of Lilavati cursing, and by now, attracted by Lilavati's shrill scolding, a crowd had gathered to watch the fun. The women were echoing Lilavati's sentiments on the boorishness of all-male households in equally irate tones.

The older guard appraised the situation and decided that a semi-riot at the gates of the orphanage, especially if led by elderly women wielding their shoes as batons, would not be in his best interest. "Shut up, donkey!" he barked at his assistant. "Phone and tell Madam what is happening. Come back and tell me, sawdust-for-brains, what she says."

The younger guard, who was rarely called by a name other than an insult, walked jauntily off. Lilavati hid a smile before breaking into loud wailing, while beating her chest. The women gathered close, eager to hear the details of another's misfortune.

Aman decided to wait for the orphanage Madam to arrive while his mother-in-law acted like the Tragedy Queen. There was nothing else to do; the two guards were zealously blocking the entrance to the orphanage and there was no other way inside.

Lilavati was still attracting people by twelve-thirty in the afternoon. Some brought her tea, while commiserating with her. Her story became elaborate and amplified by the contributions of her audience. The Madam ranged from an evil vampire who needed to suck on fresh baby blood, *make sure you see her feet, if they don't touch the ground – or they face backwards – she's surely a witch*, or the Madam was a corrupt government employee who was paid by politicians making money from children's organs for export to Western countries.

As the stories grew more macabre, the scene grew increasingly festive, and a *tilkuta* seller stopped his cart outside the orphanage, knowing that large crowds always meant customers. When no one paid him any attention, he approached Lilavati and offered her some of his sesame seed sweets, for free of course, as she had suffered so much, and must not have had time for lunch. This earned him so much goodwill from the gathered crowd that he even made some money, despite the thieving children who made use of his back being turned for that two-minute display of corporate social responsibility.

The guards were growing tired of their villainous role in Lilavati's story, and being subjected to periodic calls of '*hai hai*' from the womenfolk.

They were showered with curses alluding to the shrinking of their manhood and drying up of their semen

– surely such ill-will from the black-tongued could only spell doom? They had smoked as many *bidis* as could be chain-smoked in the time, and felt bitter in both mouth and spirit. Then a passing performer with his monkey stopped and started to shake his small drum that went *dug-dug-dug-dug-dugdugiiii* to get the attention of the crowd. The monkey had black eyes and bared her teeth at the thieving children, but the frilly pink tutu she wore around her waist undercut the ferocity of her pose. With anklets and bracelets jangling on her limbs, she unravelled the length of the rope that tethered her to her keeper and headed for the junior guard.

The guards found their moment of catharsis. They shouted a volley of curses at the man and his monkey, demanding to know whether he thought the orphanage was funded by his forefathers so that he felt free to set up shop here? Did it all look like a big theatrical production of *Ramayana* that they would need a monkey god in the middle of it all? Maybe he just needed a good wallop to remember where he was?

It was all very entertaining for the whole crowd. Even Aman found himself grinning. Unfortunately, just then the Madam's car pulled to a stop outside the orphanage and the driver honked the horn to clear the way for the shiny black Ambassador. A funereal pall spread over the crowd. The Madam emerged from the car *(her feet touched the ground but in those clunky shoes, they might still face backwards*, some whispered), and she stood in front of Lilavati.

"This man," she pointed at Aman with a sharp finger, "is trying to blackmail me about a baby I have not seen," she told the crowd. "Maybe he had a baby, but he sold her somewhere? I am not going to give this beggar anything. He is lucky I haven't already lodged a police report. And then," her hand swept around the crowd, "he creates a public nuisance with all this crying-shying. I should have him arrested first, and then throw the whole lot of you in jail too!" She pointed at a sign that said, in grammatical Hindi, *No Loitering*, and then in English, *DON'T STAND HEAR.*

"But, but *Madamji*," stuttered Aman, then tried again in Hindi. No one was listening to him. The crowd was behind Lilavati who now stood up to her full length (which was half a head shorter than the Madam) and they were not to be silenced. A couple of young men held up their fists as if holding imaginary placards and shouted, "Down with Money Politics!" and others closer to the Madam, not knowing her name, started chanting "Orphanage Madam, *hai, hai.*" One troublemaker, well past his youth, remembered the slogan of the student movement that had catapulted this city to national headlines and yelled "*Sampoorna Kranti!*" and he was followed by the nostalgic crowd yelling "*Total Revolution!*" in one voice.

Aman felt his skin prickle with excitement. It felt like the beginning of a Gandhian movement that would move mountains. Surely the Madam would have to let them in, and then he, Aman, would scoop his baby up into his eager arms while the crowd roared its approval?

But the Madam, with her shiny car and the uniformed chauffeur, was more powerful than them all. She said, "I have said what I have to say. I am going now; all of you should also go. Bring me proof of this baby, or get prepared to grind some wheat inside a jail cell. All you blackmailers and troublemakers, I know how to deal with your type." She flicked an imperious palm in Aman's direction, "Missing baby, hah!"

As the Madam turned away, Aman heard Lilavati shouting "Wait!" in two languages at the Madam's rapidly disappearing back. The driver held open the back door as the Madam slid into the black leather seat, pressing a button that sealed the tinted window shut. The car started slowly, the driver revving the engine unnecessarily to make a point but none of the assembled people thought of lying down on the ground in its path. Instead, the toothless old fellow who had started yelling about *Total Revolution* asked Aman nervously, "Eh, Brother, you have any proof you left the baby here?"

Aman shook his head wordlessly. He felt tears clouding his eyes as the toothless man sighed, "Then you have no hope, *bhai*, not against *her*. We might as well all go home now."

As the crowd dispersed, Lilavati too dusted her sari and walked away. Aman slowly followed her, looking back at the orphanage and letting his tears fall. In a fit of pique he picked up a large stone and aimed it at the gates of the orphanage, but even that disappeared harmlessly into the dusty foliage lining the entrance.

Chapter 7

The noise of the door closing behind Lilavati and Aman had woken up his daughter, Laila. Laila did not fully understand what all the fuss was about; her baby sister, a squirmy little thing whom she had been allowed to stroke very briefly in the hospital – *she's as hairy as a kitten Ma!* – was gone. And according to the whispers, Laila's father had done something. Although what he had done wasn't very clear to Laila, especially as her mother had slapped her away when Laila had asked, "Is what Nani saying true? Did... someone... bury my sister?" The foreigner must have had something to do with it. Otherwise, why was she even here?

Laila sat up and looked around for the familiar bulk of her grandmother, but could see only her little sister sleeping alone. No one else was in the room. She opened the door to clean her teeth outside, spitting rivulets of white into the murky brown drain that flowed below the house.

The morning air was cool. The cawing of the gathering crows mingled with the sleepy gossip of the line of people gathered near the door of the Mother Dairy with large aluminium and plastic receptacles to gather their morning milk. Last night's drama was still a matter of some discussion, and she could see a woman angrily jabbing at the air in the direction of their front door. The woman she was speaking to caught Laila's eye and hollered, "Eh, Laila!"

Laila quickly slipped next door. She stared at the source of all the trouble for a few seconds and then viciously yanked the curtains wide open.

*

Iris woke up immediately. The sun coming through the open slats beamed directly onto her face as she covered her eyes with a tired arm, squinting at her watch. She had slept for only three hours. Groaning softly, she slid deeper into what was surely the scratchiest rope hammock in the world. Then she remembered where she was and sat upright. There was no Maitri to be seen. Instead, there was a little girl, perhaps about five years old and quite skinny, squatting on her haunches by the bed. It was amazing how fiercely such a small child glared. As Iris blinked sleepily, she remembered the child from last night. "Hey, Laila," she called out in greeting.

In response, Laila picked her nose, twisting her forefinger in with great determination until she got a wad of snot out, which she flicked towards Iris.

Iris squeaked her outrage, "Hey!" Laila continued with her malevolent scowl. Iris may have grown up in the Indian community back in Ohio, but this was only her second trip to India and people here behaved differently. Women in India (or what she had seen of them at close quarters with their loud wailing and thumping of forehead and gargling of spit) were nothing like the Indian moms that she knew in Lima, Ohio.

Mrs Mehra (soon to be her mother-in-law) acted like she didn't even have any orifices, let alone release anything out of them. Iris looked at Laila and wondered if the child might bite. There was a feral scuttling on her little haunches that Iris was unlikely to be able to replicate. The child scurried closer, her toes splayed for support. Iris fingered her money-belt, hoping to find a packet of gum to bribe the little snot-flicker. She held it up and examined its contents in the sunlight. No passport — she knew that was in her purse on the train. No contact lens solution but there was a small bottle of rewetting drops – her day-and-night lenses had better hold out. No glasses either. And definitely no cellphone. It felt as if part of her was missing.

She glanced at the child who had come closer and was practically sitting under her bed. Then Iris discreetly counted the seven currency notes: Two 500s, two 100s, one 50 and two 20s. She felt for the coins and fished out some two rupee and one rupee coins, as well as other smaller change. This meant that she had about 1300 rupees. That was, she calculated rapidly in her head, like, 20 US dollars. She was so screwed. Her father tipped their limousine driver more than twenty bucks and here she was, looking for a way all the way back to Delhi and Danesh, on small change.

The little snot was now so close, she could feel the breath on her knee. Iris decided to ignore Laila. 1300 rupees – how much would a train ticket cost? And how much would it cost to call her father long distance? Her parents were unreachable in their Himalayan retreat with no cellphones, but perhaps she could Google the retreat and call the office? How much would an internet connection cost? Iris began to gnaw at a fingernail. Where could she possibly go for help? Even Dr and Mrs Mehra were in New Delhi now, waiting to receive Danesh and Iris into an extended family welcome, to be followed by a monsoon-wedding-styled-engagement. Her friends back home… well, no-one would be of any help with anything in India.

She hung her head in her hands, imagining herself on one of those lawless Indian highways, avoiding bullock carts and trucks while trying to hitchhike. Through her laced fingers she could see the whitewash on the wall peeling in crumbly patches. The enormity of this foreign country, its contradictions and disorganisation became a whirling mass of confusion in her mind as she visualised herself, lost and unreachable, getting as dirty and sweat-stained as Aman while trying to pay off the cost of all his broken dolls, maybe selling dolls with him at Shambala Junction next to the… internet café!

Of course! There was an internet café at the station. Iris felt her fingers prickle in anticipation as she shook off her lethargy in one swift leap to the tiny sink in the corner. Her ankle, she realized, felt much better already. She turned on the tap but there was no water. An enormous red bucket held water under the sink and she used the plastic mug to slosh her face, careful not to get any water into her mouth.

The child trailed behind her, keeping a careful distance. Iris looked at the child closely. The child stared back. Iris decided to give up and look for an adult. The door to the adjoining apartment was open and she could see Roop making tea. Iris was so happy to see Roop again that she gave her a broad smile. Roop smiled back nervously as Laila rushed to her mother and stood protectively on the other side, the fierce scowl still on her face.

"I need... station. Shambala Junction?" Roop shook her head and handed Iris a cup of tea. Iris accepted the cup gratefully and sat on the floor, sipping. Her happiness lasted for fifteen minutes, until Laila left the house hoisting a tattered green canvas bag of books on her shoulder. Roop left after her, clicking the door shut behind her.

Iris sprang to the door. It was not locked and she opened and closed it easily. She was ashamed to have expected otherwise.

*

Back in Maitri's room, Iris combed her hair with her fingers, and then gingerly licked her lips to give them some shine. She stared at the tiny mirror over the sink.

Definitely a bad-hair day, but it would have to do. She inspected her fingers, checking for the grime accumulating around her nails. She needed an emery board badly, but more than that, she needed the sanitizing hand-gel that kept her sane in this bug-infested place. She closed her eyes and willed herself back into her suite in her parents' home, the gleaming bathroom filled with rows of shiny bottles that polished her from top to toe. In her mind, she walked into her sitting room with the large-screen television, then to her bedroom, up through the spiral Louisiana-inspired stairway into her beautifully-appointed bedroom, with its lilac-mauve walls and windows overlooking the garden. Iris sighed deeply. She would have to find her way back into her real life, no matter what. She needed to find a decent toilet soon.

She peered out of the door, but could not see a single familiar face. She was on her own. Which may not be a bad thing, she reflected, especially with the bizarre neighbours she had seen last night. She looked around for some paper and a pen to write a good bye note to Maitri but saw nothing; the last thing she wanted to do was to riffle through Maitri's belongings. The sun was climbing higher overhead as it got hotter. She needed to get going – if she didn't look out for herself, no one else would. The family next door and Maitri were probably too busy trying to find the baby to even care about where she was. There was the money she should pay Aman for destroying his shop, but her father would eventually look after that.

Clicking the money-belt securely around her waist, Iris walked out the door. Opposite the apartment was a makeshift tea-tent. A black water-tank labelled '*SINTEX*' propped up a flapping tarpaulin, providing shade for the charpoy that functioned as seating. Men were sitting on it, talking and smoking. A young boy, barefoot and with a metal holder with six glasses of steaming tea, was heading out of the tent.

"Excuse me," began Iris. When the boy walked right past, she shouted, "*Hey!*"

The boy wheeled around, spilling some of the hot tea on his right foot. Iris' shout also roused the somnolent men in the tent and they all sat up, staring with frank interest. The scrotum scratcher from last night, Iris was horrified to note, sauntered out of the tent, whistling a song through teeth that were arbitrarily missing. *Gross!*

Iris felt a sense of terror at the memory of this man singing obscene lyrics at her last night. He was eyeing her up and down and she felt cowed, unable to handle the crude lechery in his eyes. What had her mother told her about handling the Roadside Romeos who had plagued her mother's youth in her village? Yes, her mother would take her sandals off and wave them threateningly in the air and the menace would usually vanish. Unfortunately, this advancing Romeo gave the impression that he would grab at her sandal-wielding hand just as an excuse to hold her. She felt sick as she imagined his malodorous breath near her mouth.

An image of her clean bedroom in Ohio flashed through her mind again. She needed to find her way home. She wasn't going to turn around and go back, the only way to go was forward. Iris was still rooted to the spot, staring at her flimsy sandals, when she thought, *Not Ma… what would Maitri do now? Or Lilavati? What? What??*

Maitri had shouted obscenities at the men and made them scatter on the railway platform. Lilavati's belligerent face, the way she had toed Aman's shoulder last night, her spitting a wad of red like congealing blood, played like a film reel through Iris' memory. So Iris raised her eyes to the level of the bulge in scrotum-scratcher's pants, gave it a long lingering look, and then, sneering straight into his eyes, she spat on the ground between his feet.

Her spit wasn't red like congealing blood, but it would have to do. Iris waited, quaking inside. There was a moment of silence as the men took in this exchange, before a group of them started to laugh like a braying pack of donkeys. One even did a little stomp-dance of pure glee.

Iris looked back once as she turned and started to walk away. The scrotum-scratcher seemed dumbfounded, as if the loss of face and an insult to his manhood, this combination was too much. Then he started to sprint after Iris. Iris spun around and shouted a panicked "Get the fuck away you stupid bastard! What the fuck are you doing?" Then, in case, he didn't understand the 'f' word, she used the one spat-out word she remembered from last night's ruckus, although for all she knew, it could mean *my little pigeon.*

"Bhenchod!" she screamed in pure terror. The scrotum-scratcher stopped in his tracks, not so much at being called a sister-fucker as by the murderous fury in Iris' eyes.

By now some women dressed in saffron saris had come out and were shouting at the scrotum-scratcher too. He retreated slowly, back into the tea-tent. One young woman (she couldn't have been more than eighteen but had a baby fastened to her breast) touched Iris' arm and asked, *"Helep?"* Iris was shaking with fear and the rush of adrenalin. It took her a while to understand that she was being addressed.

"Station," she said weakly. "Shambala Junction. Taxi. Please."

The woman took her by the elbow while holding the suckling baby with the other arm and led her through a short narrow lane with stagnant drains on both sides. Iris looked back and saw the assembled men and felt victory rise like wings in her heart. She, Iris, had done it! Alone! She had made the lecherous bully back off all by herself, with no help. She felt like a superwoman, able to lob off the grenades life threw at her. Then, to make her heart sing even louder, there stood in front of them a row of yellow and black auto rickshaws gleaming like a mirage. All were empty.

Iris turned to thank the woman but she had left, and Iris could see a flutter of her sari turning the corner of the lane. Iris laughed out loud. She felt invincible; when in India, become a furious Kali. She would have to practice this Maitri-Lilavati formula. She walked purposefully to the centre of the waiting rickshaws, ignoring the drivers that followed her with cries of: "Madam, here, Sister!"

"English?" she asked in general, "Anyone speak English?"

A few men stepped up and started to speak simultaneously. She pointed at the one with the whitest hair and used a word from her meagre Hindi vocabulary. "*Chalo*, go, Shambala Junction."

Iris' few days in Kolkata had taught her that one always haggled, even if the rate was dirt-cheap. She haggled half-heartedly with the driver who quoted fifty rupees, settling for thirty-five. "*Chalo*," she said firmly, indicating with her hand that it was time to go. She felt as poised for flight as the black mynah birds perched on top of the auto rickshaw that now flapped away into the bright sky. She felt a twinge of guilt about not saying good bye to Maitri, or leaving some money, anything at all to express her gratitude, but she would deal with that later.

For now, Iris decided, she needed to find Danesh – and just go home.

Chapter 8

Iris was startled by the busy contours of the street in the sunlight. There was a bustling spillover of life entirely absent in the silence of the night; a cacophony of street horns punctuated by the deep timbre of the trucks, and over it all hovered the scent of ripe guavas. A temple forged out of marble glistened in the sun, looming large at the T-junction ahead. As the auto rickshaw thrummed at the red traffic light, the temple bells began to toll the *arati*. Iris could see the flocks of devotees, hands hovering over the holy flame, eyes closed in prayer. She saw the priests, bare-bodied except for a sacred string slung over the shoulder, sprinkling sacred water over dark hair. There were fidgety children. A stray mutt pushed at a discarded banana leaf with its nose.

Then there was the beginning of a song, a devotional *bhajan* that sounded vaguely familiar, beginning with a single male voice and growing to a cacophony of chords as the crowd joined in. Meanwhile, the bells pealed furiously.

A child cried, its wail rising above all other sounds, and Iris turned to the young woman sitting outside the temple, bouncing a fussy toddler on her knee. The child flailed her arms in the air as she curved her spine backwards, twisting out of her mother's grip. The young mother, who looked not much older than the woman who had led Iris to the auto rickshaw stand, bounced the child higher onto her shoulder. The child's wail climbed a pitch in response. Iris watched this exchange with detachment, waiting for the stalled traffic to move again. Why did these women become mothers at all? It seemed such a tedious, messy and unsanitary pastime. Looking after a thankless brat would not be her choice – ever.

She felt her heart begin to race. *Stop it*, she told herself, *that kind of attitude is why Aman could abandon his baby*. A little girl who may be lying in a field somewhere now… the nightmare of last night came whirling back again. Being so rudely woken up by that malevolent little girl had given her no time to think, but now, sitting in this rickshaw alone, the images of the night swamped her mind. The temple bells began to chime the final stanza as the voices in prayer rose above the din. Iris' eyes closed of their own accord for she knew this drill: *If the temple bells toll as you approach, the gods are waiting for you. Ask for anything you want and your wish will be granted.*

This was, clearly, the time to ask for salvation. With the divine channels wide open, Iris took a deep breath and found herself mumbling fervently, her eyes squinting closed: *Please, please, dear Gods and Goddesses, please let the baby be found before something terrible happens to her.* Her eyes flew open as she felt the auto rickshaw moving again. There was a flash of incredulity; where had *that* prayer come from when she should be praying for her own rescue? Usually she was not at all religious – when stranded at Shambala Junction last night, her first instinct had been to cry out for her father instead of calling on God. When did she start to care about this baby she had never even seen? Or was it just guilt? At fleeing her debt to the people who had helped her so graciously last night, whom she was leaving without a good bye… after accepting their hospitality?

The auto rickshaw stalled again as people began to cross the street: women in iridescent saris carrying children on hips; men dragging children with sudden jerks as they loitered by the wayside; beggars trailing the retinue with imploring palms. Everyone seemed to be shouting, begging, and scolding at once. Iris jammed her fists into her ears against this human din as she felt the beginnings of a slight nausea. She concentrated on the bouquets of night jasmines at the flower stall outside the temple, next to gaudy marigolds and wilting roses, to clear her mind of all thought. But the heavy incense from the queen-of-the-night jasmines washed over her like a memory – these were flowers she knew, although she was smelling them for the first time in her adult life. She felt an intense sensation of *déjà vu*.

Perhaps she was stranded in Shambala for a reason? Iris felt an immediate irritation; if she didn't pull herself together and do something now to get back to her old life, she could be stranded in Shambala forever. But what if she hopped on a train and was unable to ever find Maitri again? Or Aman, whose shop she had completely trashed last night? Surely, she could not leave Shambala without an address for Maitri or Aman, even if a train to Delhi was waiting at the platform.

When she had first mulled over finding the internet café, it had crossed her mind – *if a train was leaving for Delhi right then, she should just jump on and try to find Danesh or the US Embassy* – but it seemed unconscionable now that she, Iris, could think about leaving Shambala without compensating these people who clearly had so little.

Aman was a father, and just like her own father; surely he would not give up until he had found his child again? That thought made her feel better, yes, even if everyone else gave up, she knew her father would never stop looking for her. She refused to believe that Aman had harmed the child in any way. Her heart started hammering again and she forced herself to breathe deeply. Maybe the temple bells were asking more of her than she had asked of the gods. Besides, she reminded herself, she had only twenty-eight dollars.

Danesh would come back, she was sure of it, back-tracking through the train route searching for her, so if she went searching for him at the same time, they would probably miss each other. It would be smarter to stay put here and let herself be found. But Danesh had such a terrible temper, and could be such a problem... he needed to be *managed* frequently. It would be better to use her money to Google the Ashram where her parents were. Poor Ma and Dad, they would worry so much. And Danesh, especially temperamental Danesh, was probably batshit crazy by now.

She wished she were back in Ohio, back in her driver's seat of the McLaren, breezing along a road which gleamed like tin into the far horizon. Where there was an easy solution to all problems. Iris remembered a story in *India Currents* some time ago about baby-trafficking; if this was a case of baby-trafficking, American dollars could only help the situation. She had to figure out the cheapest way to contact her parents.

*

Unsure of being able to direct a different driver back to Maitri's home, Iris asked this auto rickshaw to wait, promising him a hundred rupees but not paying him anything yet. *He must be fleecing me*, she thought as she walked away – *just look at that grin, and I haven't paid him a cent.*

Being back at the station was dispiriting. She loitered near the ticket counter and stared at the timetable for trains going to various parts of India. No mention of prices anywhere. This place was clearly very rural, with none of the easy English sprinkled into conversations she had heard in Kolkata. With her limited Hindi it would be a cycle of queues and waiting, just to get information.

Iris walked past the sign that advertised 'Rs 20/hr' and climbed gingerly down a set of narrow stairs into the internet café. It was stifling hot and table fans merely redistributed the humidity. She sat down at an empty terminal and a young man silently handed her a torn piece of paper with the time scribbled in green ink. It was 11:42, Indian time. Iris' fingers tapped at the keyboard furiously. She logged on and opened three chat programs simultaneously, searching for someone now online. The computer whirred and whined, then froze into silence. She did an alt-control-delete and sighed, signalling to the young man with the green pen. He typed in his password again and the machine blinked to life. This time, she opened Google and held her breath. *Ashram Himalaya*, she quickly typed. It brought up 1,460,000 results. She went to Google Voice and typed in a text to Danesh's American mobile phone. Maybe he'd think about checking it soon:

> *In some café in Shambala and hv no money but m staying with some nice ppl. Come back to Shambala.*

She thought for a minute.

> *Staying with Maitri (bookseller?). And Aman (doll-seller). Both at Railway Station. No address. No phone number.*

There was a sound like a giant sighing and the room went dark, all the screens blinking into a central point of disappearing light. Iris groaned. She had no idea how long this blackout would last. She had made contact with no one. If Danesh was looking for her, how would he know where to begin?

The internet man who was shining a torchlight into a gurgling generator waved her away impatiently when she approached to ask him how long the blackout would last. Iris realized that making contact with Danesh or her parents would be impossible today, especially as the other customers all started to flock out of the café. She stepped into the teeming railway station and looked around. By some miracle, if Danesh had backtracked to Shambala, they might meet now. She felt a crazy hope rise as she scanned the hordes for his familiar shirt or the jaunty edge of his cap. Nothing.

The chances of Danesh being here now, at this exact time, and then actually finding each her in this mass of humanity, she realized, was infinitesimal. Feeling despondent, Iris wandered around until she found the spot where Aman had sat last night. No sign of Aman either. Instead, there was an unfamiliar bookseller with lurid magazines, his display full of buxom breasts popping out of tight bodices and the illustrated *Kama Sutra* in various languages, including English. The drone of voices, the low chug of trains departing and arriving, the clang of metal wheels on railway tracks, the public announcements followed by stomping crowds... all this whirled into a mass of confusion and Iris sank into the edge of a grimy lamp-post so that she could lean on something.

*

As soon as the auto rickshaw dropped her back at the mouth of the dingy lane, Iris felt her stomach rumble noisily. She hadn't eaten or drunk anything since the morning tea and it was now past five in the evening. She had spent a fruitless day at the station, the internet café was still dead during her three visits, and she had shuttled back and forth from the rickshaw stand requesting the driver to stay a little longer instead of disappearing with another customer. She had bought a *puri* from the vendor hawking food, but one look at the runny potato curry made her think of diarrhoea and she had given the food to a beggar.

She had also waited outside the Station Master's office to ask for help, along with a long line of people. The Station Master, she was finally told by a porter, he had been called away for a family emergency and may not be coming back today.

When she got back, Maitri's house was locked. The sky was darkening when Iris opened the door to Aman's house to find Roop sitting on the floor. Her daughters were nowhere to be seen. No Aman or Lilavati either. But Roop looked up and smiled briefly, as if Iris' reappearance was anticipated. She had a tattered sari of soft muslin that she was tearing into long pieces. Iris sat on the bed and watched, bemused, until she realised that the thin cotton bricks that Roop was now stacking away were her sanitary napkins, and the long rolls of stained cloth drying outside, which she could see from the window even though they were hidden by some wild shrubs, were freshly washed.

Gross. Then Iris felt immediate remorse. She was unable to understand even the minutest detail of what was going on around her and she could not help Roop, who must still be bleeding from the delivery. She thought of the women under Dr Mehra's care in St. Joseph's Hospital in Ohio. Iris had been a volunteer for a couple of summers there, to meet the community-service requirements of her prep school. She had walked the halls in her cheerful lime green uniform, bringing magazines for women who later gave birth on four-poster beds with hidden stirrups, then sat on ornate rocking chairs to breastfeed their newborns.

And here was Roop, childless and bleeding, with no one except clueless Iris to help. Had she even eaten anything the whole day? The door swung open.

Lilavati stomped to the corner where the earthenware pot of water was stored, grabbed at a stainless-steel tumbler so that the dish clanked a sharp metallic note and drank in the liquid in furious gulps. Aman collapsed in a corner of the room, head in his hands.

Maitri followed the two of them in and closed the door, "Where were you?" Maitri shouted at Iris immediately. "With this missing baby, I have no time to look for another lost person! I came back after teaching, then I came back again after asking around for someone who works at that orphanage... wasting time only, back and forth, back and forth, looking for you! The tea-shop man said you had left in the morning and did not come back..."

Iris was taken aback, but felt Maitri's concern under the harsh tone. Roop had begun to keen in a corner, a sound of utter misery.

"I was at the railway station. At the internet café. I looked for you and Aman."

"You contacted your parents? Your husband? Someone is coming?"

Iris shook her head miserably. "There was a power cut..."

"Iris," Maitri said, "I know you want to find your family and go home. But I have been trying to find the baby, and when I came back in the afternoon and found the door of my house open and no one inside, I thought something happened to you also." She paused and took a deep breath. "We will help you find your family. Promise. But first we need to find this baby."

Maitri exchanged a quick glance with Lilavati, "We need your help."

Lilavati banged some dishes down and came towards them. "Tomorrow," Lilavati ordered Iris, "you go to the orphanage. Alone. You say you want to adopt a newborn baby girl. Take your passport…"

"My passport is on the train," interrupted Iris. Gathering up her courage, she said, "I need to go to the station again tomorrow, to a computer…"

Lilavati looked disgusted. "Later. Trains come every day and computers are chained to the desks. You have to help us find the baby before it's too late."

Maitri told Lilavati, in Hindi, "Slow down. You're frightening the girl." Iris looked away and saw that Roop was shouting at Aman, who was skulking in the corner. She continued her verbal assault even as the two little girls slunk into the room and sat by their parents. Iris stared at the miserable family. *Too late?* What had they discovered today?

"You couldn't bring the baby back today?"

Lilavati scowled, "Do you see a baby in this room, hahn? Don't ask stupid questions!"

Maitri sighed deeply and shot Lilavati a warning glance. "I think this plan may work. Doesn't matter about the passport. Speak Amereekan. Say you want to help poor girl babies, that sort of thing. Tell them you are leaving next week, you are barren, medically certified infertile, you have only one week and you can pay for this. Whatever you need to say, say, understand? We need proof that the baby is there, and then we can get the police and lawyers

78

involved. Without proof, we can do nothing. You know anyone who has adopted girl baby from India?"

Iris shook her head. "Doesn't matter," said Maitri. "You must act. You look rich. Shake hands with the Madam and let her see how soft your hands are."

Iris looked on silently as Lilavati went to a steel cupboard, which opened with a creak. She threw a folded sheet of cloth and a grey singlet on the bed. "Take off all your clothes; I will wash them. Rich Americans smell very clean. I have to buy some five-star soap – you have money?"

Iris hesitated. She wanted to explain that she had less than a thousand rupees after her trip today, but Lilavati threw up her hands. "Don't waste time! Babies are sold here and then cut up so they can beg for their masters."

And Maitri interjected, "We need to act *fast*, Iris."

Lilavati narrowed her eyes as she saw Iris still hesitating. "Or don't do anything, yes. Just leave now. Yes, leave this house and go, go, just go away, back to your rich husband. Go find a police station and beg for help, spend the night there and see how they take care of you!"

Iris stood immobile, feeling bullied by someone she had earlier felt so safe with. Lilavati was enraged beyond reason and if these women threw her out, where would she go? But Lilavati was not done. "I am thinking that if we are wasting our time helping you, we will never find our baby. You are *too much* wasting our time, for Maitri also and me. Leave if you want, go… go right now." And Lilavati marched to the door and held it open for Iris.

Iris could see the vicious people outside the door, that scrotum-scratcher and people like him, all those people who didn't speak English... and Delhi was miles away. She expected Lilavati would push her out the door forcefully any moment now. She felt her hands trembling as she fished out a one hundred rupee note and held it out to Lilavati, who had started putting on her slippers. Lilavati's voice softened and she looked away. "Go and change. Your clothes must dry by tomorrow morning and it's getting dark. Take everything off."

They were distracted by a loud argument. Roop held a nylon bag in her hand, one of those cheap zippered baguettes. It bulged at the seams and she had not been able to entirely close the zipper. She struggled with that now, as Aman shouted in Hindi for her to stay.

Roop ignored Aman. She grabbed her younger daughter and hoisted her on a hip, then slung the bag over her shoulder. With a quivering forefinger, Roop called for Laila. Laila shook her head and said 'No' in Hindi. Roop let out an angry whoosh of breath and turned on her heel. She shouted at Lilavati rapidly before heading out of the door. Aman followed, still pleading with the back of her straightened spine. Finally, he caught hold of her dangling hand, but Roop swung the bag at him with a fury that made him draw back. Tears streamed down her face. Maitri made a movement towards Roop, but was stopped by Lilavati's hand on her shoulder.

"Roop is leaving for my cousin's house... not too far away." She shrugged, "Maybe now she'll be rid of this useless pumpkin she married. He will try to bring her back, but, as usual, he will be able to do nothing."

"You and I have work to do, Maitri," Lilavati said. "*We* will have to find Roop's baby." Then she turned to Iris, "After, that, I promise, we will find your husband."

The door clicked shut behind Lilavati. Iris sat down on the ground, clutching at her new clothes and eyeing Maitri warily. They expected her to bathe in that filthy bathroom with the damp walls and slimy ground? She hugged her legs and buried her head into her knees. She felt cowed into a situation that she was free to walk away from, but couldn't. She would just have to suck it up and see where life took her next.

Chapter 9

On the other side of the city, inside the Shambala International Hotel, a Canadian woman was waiting by the phone nervously to complete a deal. When Vidyut had called early in the morning, Emily instantly rolled to the edge of the bed and grabbed at the phone. She was ready to leave in a minute if required.

"Congratulations," sang Vidyut.

"You have the baby?"

"Oh yes, a newborn girl!"

As he chuckled through the phone, Emily could feel the reassurance in his heartiness. It was still so scary. Even though she knew she would be seeing a baby, a tiny non-judgmental being, she still believed in the vibes of the first meeting. She had always believed in love at first sight.

"When? I mean what time should I come?" She could hear the shuffle of papers.

"This afternoon is good. About three?" The time in-between stretched like a chasm, but Emily said good bye and put the phone down. Vidyut had kept his part of the bargain. Now it was up to her, Emily, to make it happen.

She fell back into the comfort of the king-sized bed and thought, *My baby!!* Her head was woozy, like she had gulped down a heady cocktail too fast. She tried to relax now, to ready herself for the most important experience of her life, and she took in some deep breaths. Breathe in for four counts, hold for four, release for four, hold for four… and repeat. This was *it*. The culmination of months of soul-searching, and finally, a baby girl was available. Although she had been waiting for this call for the past year, it felt like an entire lifetime, this endless waiting.

When had this craving for a baby completely taken over her life, eating into her every waking thought? She had worked her way up from a journalist to a well-known features editor in a leading Toronto daily, and her work had been, for a long time, all she needed. There had been a very brief marriage lasting less than seven months before the acrimony. Post-divorce, Emily had written a series of articles about the importance of aunts and other womenfolk in the lives of babies, 'it takes a whole village' and that sort of thing, while surrounding herself with various nieces and nephews and a few young cousins. Then the economy tanked, and with it came the Big-Scandal. She had commissioned a blind linguist, one who had earned a doctorate in phonetics from McGill University, to do a story on the vanishing language of a tribe in Peru. He was gifted in his field, as his sense of hearing allowed him to faithfully distinguish sounds in a way that was almost impossible for other adult ears, and she had relied on him, with his stellar academic credentials, without checking up regularly as she was supposed to do. Especially when the story broke about this endangered tribe that lived close to the earth, populated by people who needed little and craved even less, she had been overwhelmed by the tweets and comments of readers wanting to shed their consumerist selves and live as simply as the people this linguist described. It was heady, this congratulatory fame. The morning news shows had picked up the story, then there were fundraisers to promote education among the children of this tribe and finally the humanitarian tourism started, initiated by a group of college kids in Seattle who saw this as their opportunity to 'be the change' in the world.

As soon as the college kids arrived in Peru, things started to unravel. It became clear that the tribe was not as impoverished as painted. And that the linguist was channelling much of the money that was supposed to go into building schools and humanitarian aid into his own pockets. He had signed on with a major publishing house to publish a book titled *Seven Syllables for Sweet*, and the promotional book trailer, with rosy-cheeked children surrounding the blind linguist in Peru, was already on YouTube.

A movie deal was said to be in the offing. Emily, as the features editor, became the scapegoat. The public lynching of a young female journalist (Bimbo Bitch!) attracted more tweets and comments than the feeble attempts of the media to censure an established male scholar, especially one who was disabled.

She was vilified nationwide as news anchors scrambled for sound bites on journalistic ethics on both sides of the border. *Saturday Night Live* did a funny skit lampooning an editor greedy for headlines at all cost, and Kimmel spoofed her on his late-night talk show.

The public outcry against her became so unbearable that Emily had to flee Toronto. That was five years ago. Emily now lived in a small community of three thousand people north of Edmonton, near her parents and a sister. In this small town the crazy job deadlines melted away. No one cared about who she was, or who she knew, or that she had been in an epic scandal; this community had ties going back for generations.

Young mothers with babies in the park gave their children to Emily to hug and hold for as long as she wanted; she was one of their own and felt an immediate kinship. She also started reassessing the priorities in her life as she fell in love with the weight of those little beings in her arms. Maybe it was the call of her womb, the ticking clock; it was not something she could rationalize.

In her 20's, the old Emily had written controversial articles about how motherhood was completely over-rated; now in her late 30's the new Emily cringed at the thoughts that she had once completely subscribed to. The men in this tiny town fell short of her city ideals; they were too slow here, too conservative, and when the gynaecologist gave her the news about her infertility (it wasn't completely unexpected at a time when everything was going so wrong), Emily decided she didn't need a man to complicate her life; she would bring up an adopted child on her own. This village was a great place to rear a family. It had no large malls, but it did have a great organic store, next to a coffee house on the main street where you waited for an hour if there were two people already in line. No one minded. Everything was hand-ground and conscience-filtered.

The thought of a child had taken firm root, egged on by the advice of family and friends who pitied her loneliness in a town of families. Being unable to conceive her own child also made Emily an expert on infertility as she trawled all her resources for a cure.

Emily was already a member of a church group, and she found herself playing with adopted children, many of them from China. Some of the adopted children had learning difficulties; a few had physical challenges as well. They were the discards of their own societies, now being brought up in loving Canadian homes. She decided to adopt a healthy female child from a part of the world where girls were not valued. The church had pitched in to help and the group had been wonderful with the fundraisers and bake-sales. Emily vowed to make sure that the baby wouldn't feel too foreign. Thankfully, even her little bit of suburbia was getting quite cosmopolitan; the nearby Honda plant brought enough Japanese families into the area so they had great judo and sushi. Through sleepless nights just thinking about the baby, she planned to have her baby girl enrolled in judo classes as soon as possible – a girl couldn't ever be too prepared. Her current life, one that had threatened to stretch into a lifetime of dullness with no prospect of companionship ahead, throbbed with meaning again.

By eleven in the morning, with still another four hours to wait, Emily thought she would go crazy. She had to leave the empty hotel room immediately. Emily tried to enjoy the light filtering through the intricate filigree work of the *jharokha* as she sat in the lobby, waiting for the concierge to put her in a car headed for the tourist attraction of Shambalasisa. Three o'clock in the afternoon still seemed a long time away as her mind spun around a single *tick-tock* track.

My. Baby. Finally. Here. Three. O. Clock. She needed something to fill the time. She was also here on an assignment, to write a blow-by-blow account of her experience of adopting an Indian baby, but she was too excited to scribble notes right now. She was in this beautiful hotel on an expense account but she didn't want this luxury for too long. This unexpected pampering was stifling when she only wanted her baby in her arms to take back to Canada. Emily sighed and took a sip from the glass of guava juice the concierge had offered her while she waited for her car to arrive. Hotel Shambala International was the best in town and seemed to be filled with the Japanese tourists who had arrived last night. The main group looked like geriatrics, but there was a lone young Japanese woman, who was herding them together while smiling with excruciating politeness.

Emily tried to watch them with the idle curiosity of the other hotel guests as they milled around the restaurant but her mind refused to stay in the present. Shambala had the effect of making anyone feel that nirvana was within reach; perhaps a day away, perhaps a week, but definitely soon and she, Emily, knew it was here. She looked anxiously up at the intricate patterns on the ceiling (beautiful peacocks in full plume) and hoped that the wait to take the baby home would not be long.

Emily had no idea where she was going and absently listened to the music in the car. She had already called her parents four times today and assured them that it was OK that she had come alone. Which it was; her parents would have found it difficult in India. There were the beggars everywhere, ragged children with hair as brown as the dust swirling at their feet, and they followed her around relentlessly. It was heartbreaking.

Emily finally reached the top of the Shambalasisa, where Buddha had preached his fire sermon. She had expected to feel a sensation of being close to Christ, Sermon on the Mount and all that, but she looked out at the parched valley with distant peaks and wondered how people managed to live in such desolation for such long summers. The sun must have felt as fiery then as it did now and she could imagine the one thousand former fire-worshipping ascetics all gathered here, burnt as brown as the people gathered on this hilltop, all drugged by this intense heat, listening to the One Who Attained Nirvana. She could feel the heat in soporific waves; everything shimmered slightly, as if seen through wavering smoke. The phone rang in her handbag. It was Vee.

"Is everything all right?"

Emily could not bear to even say hello, her heart was thumping so hard in her chest.

"Relax, Emily!" She felt her tension dissolve at the smoothness of his voice. "Everything's fine. I'll see you at the gate of the orphanage at three in the afternoon, just confirming that. You have a ride?"

Relief flooded through her as she found herself jabbering her thank-yous, multiple times, explaining that now, when she was so close, she expected only bad news if he called. "OK, Emily, I won't call you again. Just be there, OK, on time?"

"You betcha." She clicked her phone shut and picked up a brochure as she walked towards the *Alu-kachalu* seller. Looking with curiosity at the pile of potatoes and tamarind chutney and the smaller containers with black salt, chili powder and cumin seeds, she pointed wordlessly at the ThumsUp bottle and held out a note in payment. The dark cola slid down her throat in delightful tickles as she opened the brochure and read the translated excerpt from the Fire Sermon:

> *Brothers, all is afire. What is afire? The sight, the shapes; the iris is afire. Knowledge is afire, connections are afire, and whatever is filtered through the iris – bliss and bitterness, or neither bliss nor bitterness, that too is all afire. Afire with what? Afire with the rage of ardour, the scorch of hate, the flame of fallacy. Afire, I say, with being born, growing old and dying, with grief, sadness, misery and misfortune and mourning.*

The group of children who were following her mimed their hunger by rubbing their naked stomachs. Emily bought five packets of biscuits from the vendor sitting by the roadside and distributed the packets, trying not to look at their small faces. She continued reading:

> *Seeing this, the discerning devotee grows disillusioned with sight, disillusioned with shapes, disillusioned by the iris. And whatever is filtered through the iris, felt as bliss and bitterness, or neither bliss nor bitterness, all that too is disillusionment. Disillusioned, one becomes detached. Through detachment, one is fully released. With release, there is understanding.*

Emily raised her head. She could see the motley group of children heading for the next tourist bus pulling in. They had no time for play; it was work for them as long as tourists like her showed up. She felt her eyes prickle; so many children with miserable lives. Too many children who could not be adopted into better lives.

Beside a square white enclosure it was all brown on the hill. The rough-hewn rocks scattered on the dusty ground made room for brown shoots to limply wave in the wind. Her skin tingled with a tragic epiphany; on this hill, pregnant with religious history, she could see absolutely no signs of life.

She told herself to stop being silly. Vee had called, the baby would be in her arms in another hour. All would be well. But the feeling pursued her. Sitting in a traffic jam on the way to the orphanage, Emily could only think about all the things that could go wrong. The gates of the orphanage would be locked by the time she reached it. Her lateness would look like disinterest and Vee would become uncooperative. While she was in this stalled car, another prospective family would visit the orphanage and fall in love with the same baby... Emily wanted to weep.

She craned her neck out of the window again to check the traffic and breathed in the polluted smog. Lines of cars were stuck at an ancient fortified gateway and there was a deafening noise of horns. She felt like screaming. Her baby was waiting for her at the orphanage and she was going to be so late. She couldn't believe how restless she had been, and how unbearable the hotel had seemed, leading to this ill-timed trip to Shambalasisa.

Chapter 10

The car from Hotel Shambala International came to a screeching stop right in front of the gates of the Wings of an Angel Home for Destitute Children, creating a line of commuters hollering abuse at the tinted windows. The uniformed chauffeur stepped out and opened the door, and Emily rushed out. The heat and dust smacked Emily in the face immediately. She held her breath until she felt slightly dizzy, then, seeing Vee, she rushed towards him.

"So sorry I'm late, Vee, the traffic was backed up all the way from Shambalasisa!"

"Hello, hello, hello," said Vidyut genially, "I'm glad you're here... finally!" He guided her elbow towards the door as Emily blinked nervously, "Let's go in."

He steered Emily through the long corridor which had a lingering antiseptic odour. Emily could not see a single picture anywhere on the long bare walls. Her anxiety peaked as they stepped into a high-ceilinged room with a number of cribs placed tightly together, where five ayahs scurried about in flapping saris, clearly overworked. The noise of wailing and hiccupping children was relentless.

"Wow. How do they fall asleep here?" asked Emily.

"They're already used to it. Like the men sleeping outside on the pavement, in bright sunlight, with the noise of the traffic? A bit like that." Vidyut shrugged.

Emily took a deep breath. This was the culmination of eleven months of waiting; for LifeSavers to get the referral and then the seemingly endless wait for the Indian authorities to pre-approve a foreign adoption. Before all that had been mountains of paperwork: forms, educational transcripts, tax records, financial statements, medical reports... then came the home visits, where strangers opened her bathroom cabinets and her refrigerator. For a while, Emily felt she was starring in a particularly bad reality show. Now the immigration formalities (if things went according to Vee's plan) would be short and the baby could be home in eight weeks. She hoped she could keep the baby with her until she could get on the flight home.

It had already been eleven long months of priming herself and her extended family for this new addition to the brood, hauling herself out of depression after each setback and convincing herself that this agony would be worth it. And before all that, there were the long monologues with her sleepless self through long nights, justifying this decision in economic and personal terms.

The baby wasn't even born when she had started to dream of her and Emily felt as if it was her desire alone which had brought this particular baby into being. There was no way that any baby they brought to her today would not be perfect. Still, Emily felt all wound up. She thought of all the babies she had held and how good that had felt, especially the little ones in church…

An elderly woman was walking towards them and Emily smiled weakly as the woman pushed up her glasses on a thick beak-like nose. She briefly wondered why anyone would wear a high-collared black blouse in this heat; most of the Indian women here showed bare skin at their midriff and neck, but this woman was completely sheathed from ankle to toe.

Vidyut took the woman's hand in a brief clasp, "Ah, here's Shabnam. She runs the orphanage that found your baby."

Emily smiled briefly at Shabnam before her journalistic instincts kicked in. "Not this orphanage? Why didn't we just go there then?"

It was eight months after signing a contract with LifeSavers that an Indian colleague had scanned and sent her a whole slew of unflattering articles from Andhra Pradesh. The Indian journalist had initially been reluctant to hand over all the information to Emily (the adoption process had been set in motion), but she had insisted on seeing the proof. The articles accused Vidyut of baby-trafficking (in three languages), but it had already been eight months and Emily was heavily invested, both emotionally and financially, in LifeSavers India. Besides, Vidyut had won the court case and explained that it was a highly politicised bid by Lakshmy Mittal to run for public office – 'See, it is so localised it's only in the AP media, none of the Delhi or Mumbai papers will carry such lies.' So she had done some research on this on her own, found no pending cases against him in North America, and decided to go ahead with this. As a precaution, Emily had also checked with the US Consulate in India and they were fully backing Vidyut in the court case. She was told as an idle aside (strictly off the record of course) that officials of the World Bank had pulled strings with the Indian State Government reliant on foreign aid. By this time, she knew Vidyut and trusted him, and the need for a baby had become a physical ache in her body.

She had let it go. But now, she felt her head prickle with tension as Shabnam and Vidyut exchanged glances and spoke at the same time.

"They are sister orphanages… and it'll be rush hour soon…" began Shabnam.

"It's the same organisation. The other orphanage is more troublesome to visit in this traffic…" Vidyut trailed off. "Look Emily, here's the baby."

Emily whirled around to see an approaching ayah. Her face softened as she held her arms up slightly, waiting for the baby to come to her.

*

Shabnam inspected this foreign woman from head to toe. The woman's flaming red hair was quite distinctive, otherwise she was the usual type, middle-aged and barren, spreading to a slight roll of fat around the waist. Shabnam had handled this type before and babies harvested from the Lambadas were the easiest to place with these women; the Lambadas were nomads found all over India, with fair skin and Caucasian features. Their community had its cultural and economic life destroyed by the march of modern India, and unable to keep up, the Lambadas were in a cycle of poverty and hunger where it became easier to sell their children than raise them. Unfortunately, the government had clamped down on this niche market quickly. Now Shabnam hunted for poor and pregnant women who already had one or two daughters. The mother had nothing to negotiate with; for as little as five hundred rupees *(which would be a latte break for this rich bitch)* the new-born girls were bought for her by her touts.

She had to pay the touts six thousand rupees per baby, but she made much more than ten times that amount in the final transaction. Mothers who tried to reclaim their babies were dealt with swiftly; Shabnam just told them to get out and breed another one.

Shabnam clenched the mobile phone in her hand and hoped that this would be over very quickly. When the call had come from the guard at Anath Aashray, the other orphanage, about a gathering protest at the gates because of the child that this white woman was now cradling in her arms, it had taken her by surprise. She had first dismissed the problem, knowing that the senior guard was especially prone to exaggeration. The baby's father was persistent, which in itself was not unusual, but he had been able to whip up local support, which was always trouble in their business. Shabnam had to rush to the orphanage and squelch the problem immediately, then turn around to reach here in time. So much to-ing and fro-ing over so little had given her a headache in this heat.

Shabnam looked at her watch impatiently. She had to get back to her orphanage and get to the bottom of this, but she knew she had to give Emily time to bond with the child.

This one, unfortunately, was a journalist; she could raise an international media ruckus if things went wrong. But if things went well, the publicity would be worth its weight in gold. She congratulated herself on her instinct to have the baby moved to this home yesterday evening, just in case the father returned later in the night along with his male relatives to forcibly take the baby home. She had dealt with him so decisively earlier today that she doubted he would come back again, especially as he had no proof of ever leaving his baby with her. Better to be safe than sorry, she told herself. Red-hair looked like a pushover. She looked the type that would be willing to pay a lot of money to get this rabble-rousing baby out of the country as soon as possible.

Shabnam sat back in the loose wicker chair and asked the helper to get a *nimbu-pani* for her parched throat.

Emily was enchanted. The baby had silky soft skin and even softer hair, in tiny curly ringlets that hugged her skull. Then, while stroking the hair, she felt the soft fontanel and felt a pulse beating rapidly. Emily drew her hand away. This was a newborn child, she felt sure of it. While covering a story on Sudden Infant Death Syndrome she had held many premature and newborn babies; one didn't have to be a mother to know how a newborn felt. Surreptitiously, she loosened the swaddling to check the baby's shoulders and back. There it was, the lanugo, a fine coating of soft hair that darkened her shoulders. She checked the navel and found it wrapped in gauze – the stump had not dropped off yet.

How could they get a baby so young to prospective parents? Shouldn't the form-filling and transfer of guardianship take a couple of weeks at the very least? She had seen Indian bureaucracy as soon as she had landed at Delhi airport, and it was anything but fast. What was going on here?

Emily turned to Vidyut, "She feels like a newborn, Vee. Is she a preemie or something?"

Vidyut looked at Shabnam who turned deliberately away to reach for her glass. "She was born, um, just a week ago."

"And the paperwork has been done? Isn't there a period of time in which the parents get to change their mind?"

Shabnam said, "She has no parents."

Vidyut said simultaneously, "They died, in a bus accident. Her mother had to have a caesarean so that the baby could be born."

"So how did she come to you?"

Vidyut sighed. "Very sad case. The family was in a large wedding party travelling by a bus. Mostly all died, but an old aunt of the parents survived, and she brought her to Shabnam saying 'I can't do this in my old age, find a good home.' Very tragic."

"And Shabnam has the papers transferring guardianship from this aunt then?"

"Yes, of course." Shabnam said. "If you want, I can give you a copy today itself. We have the baby's birth certificate and the parents' death certificates, all that, everything also, we have in our records."

Emily's smile did not reach her eyes. "Must have been quite an accident – a whole bus, wow! Where was it?"

Shabnam frowned at Vidyut, then spoke slowly, lapsing into a thick accent, "All these things are happening to the poorest of our people. Tch, we have no value for life in India. Always like this; big group in small car and the driver cannot steer properly also, so sad. Off a hill in Jhumritalaiya, very far, in Bihar. Very difficult to reach."

Emily looked at them both silently.

"But," Shabnam continued, "all is in the past. Now this little girl will go to a good home and have a bright future. An all-Canadian Girl, eh?"

That was when the baby opened her puffy eyelids and looked straight at Emily. She had the most wonderful dark brown irises, flecked with black. Just as suddenly she breathed in a large sigh, twisted her pouty little lips and fell asleep again. The weight of the baby felt so right. She smelt of baby powder and laundered cotton, and when Emily stroked the side of her face, her lips rooted for Emily's finger. This newborn was a new experience for Emily. She found herself suffused with a warm glow that told her she was in love.

Vidyut stood on her right. "They've named her Piya," he said softly. "You can change it of course. It means 'beloved' in the local language. Rather a transcultural name don't you think?"

"How soon can I take her home? I want to take her home now."

Shabnam spoke up. "Today is not possible Madam, but only for you, Madam, we will process the papers in two weeks. It takes longer for non-Indian parents, you understand, it will cost a little extra. But we will try, only just for you. Until then, you can visit whenever you want, just let me know."

"Thank you," said Emily. She picked up Piya's right hand and stroked her own cheek, engrossed in the softness of this tiny being. Her body throbbed with the sheer magic of this moment. It was definitely love at first sight.

*

Later that night, Emily couldn't sleep. All she could think of was the baby and her arms ached to hold her again. Emily had gone through a phase of investigative journalism on a variety of morbid topics involving children: Sudden Infant Death Syndrome, the Medea syndrome of murderous mothers, anything that dealt with the unnatural death of babies. In the course of this year she had held crack babies and preemies, and in one instance, quadruplets who were three days old.

She knew newborn babies. The fontanel on the head, the lanugo on the back, the puffed eyelids and the umbilical cord… any of these things, even two or three of them together would not have mattered. This baby felt like she was barely out of the womb before Emily had held her.

But it didn't matter. Even if the baby were a newborn, it would be her newborn. Her daughter. After so many frustrating years of waiting and hoping, this baby would be hers, no matter what. She remembered the lovely eyes and that soft mouth rooting for her finger. The baby felt like a squiggly miracle. She didn't believe in destiny, but

India was changing her mind. This baby was definitely her destiny.

Returning to the hotel in the chauffeured car, she had slipped into her usual place in the front seat, refusing to sit alone at the back. She had been preoccupied with the baby and felt a yearning as well as a vague unease. The driver had turned on the music. A Hindi song flowed out from the speakers, the unfamiliar words jumbling into a fog of sound with one exception; the singer was saying "Piya," over and over again. Emily had turned to the driver more imperiously than she had intended and asked, "What is this song?"

"Sorry Madam. I will switch off." The driver's face was contrite as the sudden silence filled the car.

"That's not what I meant. What is 'Piya'? What is this song about... please?"

The driver spoke excellent English and was only too happy to lecture on his language and culture when given an opportunity. "You like the song Madam? 'Piya' is something like dear, darling, you know? And this song is saying '*Aaja Piya Tohe Pyar Doon*', which means 'Come to me my darling, I will love you very much'. It is a famous song by Lataji, our own Indian nightingale. This is the remix, from London. You will listen?"

The car filled with remix wails of *Don't know why, don't know how*. Emily sank back into the white cotton covers and thought, *Thank you, Jesus.*

*

Emily looked at the glowing hands of her watch in the dark; it was now 1:30 in the morning. She couldn't sleep. She reached out for her laptop and opened the page to the news reports she had bookmarked. She scanned the details about LifeSavers India and the baby Chaya case being heard at the courts now. She closed the cover of the laptop abruptly. Emily didn't believe that she was put on earth to save the naked and the homeless. She knew that maintaining her gluten-free organic vegan lifestyle was so expensive that only the wealthy of the western hemisphere could pay for such self-denial.

She could afford her lifestyle with little manual labour and supplementary pills that kept malnutrition at bay, but she enjoyed having the choice to live and eat simply, and as long as she could keep herself healthy she had neither the inclination nor the time to take on the problems of the rest of the planet.

LifeSavers India had been in trouble with the law before, but Vee was a good man, she knew it. This baby was *perfect* for Emily, and that is why Vee had found her. She should stop worrying about how a newborn baby may have come to the orphanage. There was no reasoning this want, she only knew that she, Emily, wanted the baby, this baby, and she would take her back home in two weeks. That was it. She had already told her parents about how gorgeous the baby was, how she had opened her eyes and looked right at her. She had emailed her sister about the miracle of the song on the radio.

She went down to the hotel bar and ordered a glass of champagne to celebrate signing the deal. This baby was going to be her own and if it took more money to make the wheels turn faster in India, that was the way things worked here. She would take Piya home – and she wouldn't let anyone stand in her way.

Chapter 11

Early in the morning, a young Japanese woman shepherded the Japanese tourists filing through the lobby of the Shambala International Hotel and onto the coach that would take them the short distance to the Shambalasisa Mountain. Kiku was on a Buddhist pilgrimage with her parents, but being the youngest in this group of geriatrics was definitely too much work and no fun.

Kiku watched her group milling around the Mahabodhi temple rising like a beautifully filigreed stone from the ground, with a miniature *stupa* and the spire reaching into the blue sky of a perfect day. She watched for signs of distress, someone needing the toilet or a bench to sit on, and was relieved to see that all seemed well. She had already seen the diamond throne and the holy *bodhi* tree and now stood some distance away, trying to get the best angle through the camera lens. She had finally distanced herself from the group she was with, leaving them in the hands of the Indian tour guide, and she breathed in the pervading sense of peace.

She could imagine the Buddha wandering for six full years and then finding nirvana here, right under a tree like the one she was standing below, shaded by its cool foliage. She leaned over the small railing with the sign explaining the founding of the original temple. A double flight of stairs led to the inner sanctum, but she lingered outside, focusing on the mouldings of the Buddha images set in niches along the wall.

In the distance, she could see her parents trying a sesame-seed sweet by the souvenir stand. As she focused her camera, she doubled up at the cramps in her stomach. Simultaneously, she felt her phone vibrating in her pocket. Kiku ignored the phone as she willed the cramps to subside. She hadn't felt good since this morning, yet the fellowship coordinator was still sending these urgent messages from the Netherlands. First she had texted Kiku at around 12:30 in the afternoon from the office in Leiden, and then called from Amsterdam since Kiku hadn't replied. In between the two, Kiku had managed to understand that a Swiss tourist had been gang-raped at Agra today, and coupled with the vicious gang-rape of the woman in a Delhi bus, the organization felt Kiku should come back to Leiden at once. The Institute was becoming very nervous about her roaming around the small towns of India, a lone female research scientist, especially as their funding was making her trip possible.

Kiku, who prided herself on being a Third Culture Kid at home in the world, who could walk the streets of New Delhi as confidently as Buenos Aires, who spoke four languages fluently and understood three more, well, she wasn't going to be cowed into going back without completing her research! The research would start in another week but right now Kiku, shoved by fate and filial piety to take her parents on a pilgrimage to the place of Buddha's nirvana, was in the Shambala.

The Buddha must be laughing. Kiku did not speak *this* language, she had been groped by strange men trying to tell her something quite contrary to the directions she was asking for and now the institution wanted her to cut short this long-planned trip because of *Something-Which-Might-Happen*. Hah! Kiku was not going to even try to find her way through an academic bureaucratic maze to change her plans and have to do this all over again later.

Kiku straightened up and switched off her cellphone. She walked into the temple and came face to face with the one thousand seven hundred year old image of Buddha touching the ground. She sat down in a corner to breathe deeply and calm down.

*

Half an hour later, Kiku was sitting cross-legged on a rope stool. Her stomach heaved at the sight of the yellow curry and steaming rice. All she wanted now was a plain rice ball, wrapped in the crunch of the *nori* with a tangy plum inside gummy rice. She was fed up with this greasy Indian food with its fiery spices and the runniness of it all. She had been warned about the Delhi Belly but never saw it coming until what she had thought was going to be a gentle fart had left her bottom wet. She was in the elevator going up to her room after breakfast and even though she clenched her buttocks in panic, she could feel the liquid run down her thigh. The elevator had been empty but she still felt her face prickle at the memory. She had swallowed two Lomotils and felt reduced to the level of the elemental – shit, fart, food – and the horror of an accident happening in a place so public that the shame would be unbearable.

Diarrhoea was ubiquitous in the tour group but the Indian guide, Narayan, remained relentlessly cheerful and exempt from this plague. Narayan handed out Lomotils as if they were breath mints after all meals. Some of the older tourists were now grimacing with the pain of constipation and Kiku could see one now, someone who had refused to eat, listlessly turning the prayer wheels at the monastery (one-two-three-four) and then cramping up at the pain in his stomach. This was a pilgrimage for the damned. And to think that she was going to spend another three months, even after her parents were through with the pilgrimage, to finish her research on mathematical patterns in traditional Indian folk tunes.

Kiku turned on her phone and it immediately beeped with received messages. What was the Institute's problem? She was 26 years old for fuck's sake! She would finish this project, no matter what. She could not, would not, make this trip again.

She would have to make time to go see the Station Master at Shambala Junction soon. In the confusion of their arrival, yesterday, one of the suitcases was left on the platform somewhere. The hotel staff had made some calls earlier today and apparently a similar suitcase had been logged in the early morning at the lost-and-found department of the railway station. With so many terrorists and bombings nowadays (the guy at the reception had joked) no one touched unattended suitcases anymore: *it's the best time to lose your belongings in India, Madam.* As the only young person in this group, there was no question about who would go on the quest to retrieve the suitcase.

Kiku felt another sharp cramp and doubled up in pain. It was clearly out of the question to help anyone but herself now.

*

By six in the evening, Kiku was feeling less liquescent. Her stomach and her mood had both improved. She had paid Narayan a fat tip to drop her off at the railway station and arrange to pick her up in an hour. An hour, that was it. If the bag wasn't lurking around the station in that time she wasn't going to pursue this any further.

Directed by Narayan, Kiku headed for the Station Master's office. Her obvious Japanese features cleared the way for her; she was a tourist of the East Asian variety who was expected to speak no Hindi and terrible English. The usual door-jammers decided it was best to wave her inside without trying to solicit any money. She heard voices inside and knocked loudly on the green door with the sign '*STATION MASTER*' in white letters. She didn't know how long the effects of the Lomotil would last; it was better to get this over and done with so that she could go back to her room.

A man's voice barked, "Come in!"

Kiku swung the door open and saw a fat man in a white shirt with wet transparent patches, the ribbed white singlet he wore beneath clearly outlined. He was sitting on the other side of the table. On her side was a tall young man, also Indian, who was standing up and leaning into the middle of the table, fingertips pressed down hard to make a point.

"... Somebody must have seen her! She got off the train at the Shambala stop last night and didn't get back on. She *is* here, somewhere."

He turned to look at the intruder and Kiku felt a warmth shooting through her pelvis and reaching her face. She had never, in her twenty-six years of life, seen anyone so devastatingly handsome before.

He ignored her as he took a cellphone from his pocket and gestured to the Station Master.

"I have a message from her. She's here with someone called Maitri and Aman. At a café at the railway station."

"Please sit, Madam," the Station Master invited Kiku. "Can I help you?"

"How about helping me first?" growled the young man. The Station Master and Kiku both looked taken aback at such rudeness.

The Station Master stood up. "In America," he wagged his finger at the man, "You may be screaming-shouting your *badtameezi* everywhere. Here, in India, all our clients are same-same. Like guest to our country. '*Athithi Devo*

Bhava', you know the advertisement, 'Incredible India? Our Guest is our God!'"

*

Danesh mentally hit his head against an invisible wall and counted to three. OK. This guy had obviously gone to the same hospitality school as his mom and probably had more imbecilic homilies under his belt. Now this woman had barged in and the Station Master was perspiring heavily just looking at this Japanese doll. If he went around knocking on the door of every house in Shambala for Iris, it would probably take him less time than dealing with this clammy clown.

"I am sorry," said the Japanese woman, bowing. "I interrupted. I have a problem and I am not well," she rubbed her stomach slightly, "so sometimes I have to be quick. I am very sorry," and she bowed again.

Danesh looked at her. She seemed so contrite and her voice was so low that he felt like a boor. The Station Master's glare amplified that feeling. "Please go ahead," said Danesh, still churlish. "I am not sick, so I'll just wait until I am."

The Station Master gave Danesh a smile. Then he topped up his Limca while shouting for the peon to get another. Danesh jiggled his foot and waited.

"I have a problem with a missing suitcase," began the woman, glancing at Danesh apologetically.

"Japanese? Tourist?" asked the Station Master. "You have police report?"

"No, no. You see, we got off the train in Shambala last night and we had many many bags. I am trying to find one that didn't come to the hotel with us. The hotel staff said it is in the lost-and-found?"

Danesh lost interest. How long would it take for this Station Master to find a missing bag and get back to Iris' disappearance? Earlier this morning, it had taken him a long time to realise that Iris was not on the train. He woke up to the busy clamour of Mughal Serai Junction, brushed his teeth, and it was only when the man came around with flasks of hot tea on aluminium trays that he realised something was wrong. Then another passenger told her son about seeing Iris on the platform in Shambala drinking tea. As his anxiety grew, so did the crowd around them and their suggestions. There was no point in pulling the emergency chain that was labelled *'To Stop Train Pull Chain'* and underneath, *'Fine 1000 Rupees and One Year in Jail for Misuse'*. Then the helpful passengers scoured the toilets and the bays *(all foreigners were drunken alcoholics)* in case Iris was asleep somewhere else. Finally the ticket-inspector was summoned. He checked his records; the train had stopped at Shambala Junction for eleven minutes and left at 2:46 in the morning. He shook his head sadly.

Danesh had felt the blood pumping through his head. *Where could Iris be?* She was never alone; never. This whole train idea was so dumb that it could have only come from Iris! Now she wouldn't know what to do – God! She barely spoke Hindi – she'd be a nervous wreck.

A part of him just wanted to keep going to Delhi and let her deal with the consequences of her actions for just one time in her silly privileged life. But he felt responsible for her, as he always did, and it was late in the afternoon when he had knocked on the Station Master's door at Shambala.

"We got off the train last night, on the way to Delhi. The Drut Express?" the Japanese woman was explaining. They were still talking about missing luggage?

"I am looking for a *person* who got off the Drut Express and is lost," said Danesh belligerently to the Station Master. "Time is running out. You give a missing luggage form to this lady, and while she fills it out, you find *my missing person*. OK?"

"Why are you being so rude and in a hurry only?" asked the Station Master in exasperation. "We can find both luggage and people. We are the Indian Railways."

Danesh sighed and tried again. "I am looking for someone who got off the train last night in Shambala. My friend, Iris. We were travelling to Delhi… she speaks almost no Hindi…"

The Japanese woman turned to him, "Oh, that is terrible!" She turned to the Station Master, "Yes, you must find his friend. So many bad things happening now…" She held out her hand, "… my name is Kiku."

They shook hands as Danesh introduced himself. The Station Master glowered at them both.

"We can find people *and* luggage. All is well." He turned to the woman and asked about the dimensions of her suitcase as if Danesh had never interrupted. Danesh felt a flash of fury – *why did this imbecile even have this job?* Then he realised that his fury was getting him nowhere. He tried to breathe evenly, the way he had been taught in his recent anger management sessions.

"Please read this message," said Danesh, waving his phone, "This is a message from Iris! She is with Aman the doll-seller from the railway station... and Maitri..."

"We have many doll-sellers," the Station Master said, finally reading the message, "but we will find this kidnapper. I will personally make inquiries about criminal elements. *Hari*!" he shouted.

Danesh interjected hastily, "She hasn't been kidnapped – she said she was OK and staying with nice people..."

The Station Master sniggered. "Nice people, hah! Lots of *goondas* here. I do not wish to scare tourists, but give me a photo of this missing lady, please."

Danesh took out his wallet and extracted a recent picture from the three he had of Iris.

"Pretty girl, hahn?" The Station Master stomped towards the door and shouted instructions at the guard sitting outside. "Now we wait. My man will find out who took this foreign tourist and what is happening." He opened a drawer and extended a packet of nutty biscuits towards them, "Here, have, take please. You are my honoured guests. We will find the missing luggage and the missing friend." Turning to Kiku, he asked solicitously, "Madam, you will take soft drink?"

*

It had been half an hour and the Station Master had started to ask them irrelevant questions about the state of global education and the careers of their extended families. Danesh and Kiku had looked at each other in mutual understanding and both stood up at the same time. Danesh said he should check the email at the internet café in case Iris had sent more news and Kiku said she might as well check her mail too. They told the Station Master they would be back in half an hour.

Walking to the internet café with Kiku at his side, Danesh found himself uncharacteristically tongue-tied. This petite foreigner was navigating the bureaucracy and chaos of this country to enquire about some missing luggage that was not even her own; he couldn't imagine tolerating this kind of nonsense for anything minor. He'd dealt with the Station Master with a lot less success than this poised young woman. He wanted to express his admiration but he found himself absolutely at a loss for words. The only thing that came to his mind was a Zen proverb that his judo master often quoted:

> "*When you seek it, you cannot find it*
> *Your hand cannot reach it, nor your mind exceed it*
> *When you no longer seek it*
> *It is always with you.*"

How the hell was *that* even relevant?

*

The lone internet café was easy to find. Danesh and Kiku made their way past stalls selling lurid magazines in technicolour and fended off tea boys who tried to sell them hot *chai*. Finally, they manoeuvred themselves down a narrow set of stairs and into the internet café where a generator was loudly whirring. The air was damp and unmoving. Danesh furtively swiped at the sweat on his brow with the edge of his sleeve. This place felt like the underworld. If he ever shot a movie about being in hell, this dungeon internet café would be the ideal location. He held up two fingers to ask for two computers and was given two slips of paper with the time scribbled in green ink. Then they were herded into a far cubicle with two grimy terminals. Kiku positioned herself in front of the keyboard like a perky pianist and flashed him a grin. "Good luck – I hope your friend managed to contact you again!"

He smiled grimly at her in the semi-darkness as the hourglass on the screen hovered next to the cursor interminably, then the pages formed, line by excruciating line.

There was no message from Iris. He checked his two in-boxes, Google Talk, Messenger, even Skype, yet there was no trace of Iris anywhere besides the cryptic message on Google Voice. No address or any sort of a lead. Danesh found a fist of fury drumming in his head that she probably was not trying very hard to reach out to him in any meaningful way. He could imagine a tearful Iris being mollycoddled by a bookseller and a doll-seller somewhere, completely helpless while she waited to be rescued. He heard the gentle patter of the keyboard as Kiku typed in word after word next to him, the sound fuelling his frustration. What kind of a relationship was he in that he had so little faith in his fiancée?

He raked his fingers through his sweaty hair. This airless room was getting claustrophobic.

Iris had always been a part of his life. His parents and hers had been vacationing together since Iris and he were babies but the marriage-pact between the mothers had made it clear, very early in their lives, that they were not siblings. Iris had never tied a *rakhi* around his wrist or pressed a black *tilak* on his forehead for Bhai Phota. He had cringed at this infant-betrothal, terrified that his pill-popping cheerleader-fucking buddies would find such a notion not merely quaint but positively Neanderthal. He had avoided Iris as much as possible during his teenage years so that there would be no hint of an alliance, but inexplicably, when they had returned from a holiday in Singapore and she had been about 15, she had developed an embarrassing crush on him. She had been impossible to shake off until six years ago when he had finally broken away; he married someone else.

His ex-wife was South Indian. It wasn't necessary to be Punjabi (Iris was Bengali) but he hadn't anticipated his mother's stolid disapproval, the sharp undercurrent of hostility in her dealings with his spouse. His wife had been too dark, too short, too Madrasi, whatever that meant. It also didn't help that Danesh had been so clueless when he had married, so very young. When his wife had left, eighteen months after the wedding, he hadn't been so angry as much as taken by surprise – he hadn't known how to make it right for her because he hadn't known that he was doing anything wrong.

After all that, Iris' father, Dr Sen had leaned into his ear and whispered words which had changed everything. Dr Sen's speech had slurred after a stroke, and in the hospital room he had spoken with great deliberation, "Look after

Iris for me, *beta*. The next attack will be my last." Danesh had reassured Dr Sen, mumbling in confusion, but they both knew that Dr Sen had just placed what was most precious to him under Danesh's care. And that was how, obliquely, Danesh had accepted the inevitable. There was no reason for him to push Iris away anymore; he had already tried and been found singularly inadequate. Had his love for Iris grown, as he was told it would, as a force of habit? He certainly worried about her all the time. What more could he want?

What, indeed?

Danesh clicked the tab on Messenger again, hoping that Iris, by some miracle, would suddenly be online now. There were internet cafés and mobile telephony stores at every turn in Shambala, and Iris probably had access to more than just this one cramped and humid hole-in-the-wall. He looked at Kiku from the corner of his eye. She had claimed to be sick, but she looked perfectly well, not even breaking out in a sweat in this thick humidity. She was typing something, perfectly engrossed, her brow unfurrowed. A slight smile hovered around her lips. She felt him looking at her and turned to him. He shook his head.

The Station Master, trailed by his peon, tripped into the room, barely ducking in time to miss the low ceiling at the entrance.

"Yes, we have a doll-seller, Aman," he said happily. "He thinks he is the son of our Tragedy Queen."

Danesh looked at Kiku, who looked blankly back.

"The Tragedy Queen of *Pakeezah*?" The Station Master looked sad and quoted, "'*Aap ke paon dekhe, bahut*

haseen hai. Inhe zameen par mat utariyega – maile ho jayenge...'
very romantic. You must see our Hindi movies – best in
the world..."

Danesh interrupted, looking at his watch pointedly.
"Where can I find this Aman?"

"Some days he comes, some days he doesn't. Today
he doesn't. You come back tomorrow and look. I will
help you."

"Do you have his address? Or his full name?"
asked Kiku.

"No Madam, but not to worry. This Aman is only
insane, you know, thinking he is son of Tragedy Queen
and all. Insane," he emphasized with a flourish, "but not
criminal element."

"What?" shouted Danesh, "which is worse?" Kiku
raised a restraining hand, then drew back self-consciously.

A smile hovered around the Station Master's lips as he
took in this exchange. "I have helped you as guests to my
country. Now you make police report, or you don't make
police report, it is your decision. My duty is finished." He
put his hands together in a *namaste* and turned to Kiku.
"Madam, you please check the two bags in my office, I
think one is belonging to you."

Kiku bowed. "Thank you very much. I am so grateful."

Danesh looked from the Station Master to Kiku and
wondered why she made him feel so gauche. The Station
Master started to walk away but the peon hovered around,
scratching his right palm meaningfully until Danesh took
out his wallet and handed him a note

"I have to go now," Kiku said quickly. "Good luck with
finding your friend."

"Where are you staying?"

"At Shambala International. My parents are here on a Buddhist pilgrimage… the Buddha said that anyone who makes this trip to Shambala–" she took a theatrically deep breath, "*will, at the dissolution of the body, be reborn in heaven.* So I'm piling on the good deeds."

"Ah. I don't have a hotel yet, but I'll try to ask some questions about this Aman before I find a place. Is the Shambala International any good?"

"I am staying there – it can't be all bad, can it?" She had a dimple creasing around her mouth, and her hair flounced in a silky curtain as she turned. She lifted an arm in farewell and lightly ran up the stairs, her arm as graceful as the neck of a white swan.

Chapter 12

Iris awoke to a sensation of being poked with a sharp twig. "Yow!" She squirmed to a sitting position, pulling her T-shirt down over her midriff, and turned to see Laila squatting, one bony forefinger lifted, aiming for her uncovered belly. There was the noise of clanging aluminium milk cans outside the window. Iris groaned into the pillow. "*Not again!*"

Laila was dressed to go out and her hair was neatly combed into two severe ponytails held up by two giant lemon-coloured fasteners. "*Jaldi karo!*" Laila's voice held a note of exasperation. She grabbed Iris's wrist to jab at her watch. Iris felt tension grab her chest and tighten it, hard. The orphanage! She was supposed to go to the orphanage today with Laila. She jumped out of bed swiftly and dabbed at her teeth quickly with the powdered toothpaste, her index finger working like a toothbrush as she had been taught last night.

She looked at herself in the mirror and told herself to calm down. Lilavati and Maitri had coached her for three hours last night, asking all the questions that the orphanage Madam would ask. Iris knew this was the most important acting role she would ever play – it may really save a child – and she had certainly never felt so valued for what she could do. She felt more alive than she ever had in her life.

"Be confident!" Lilavati had barked every time Iris had stuttered or hesitated before an answer. "You are very rich; *you* tell *her* what to do!"

Now, in the bright light of the day, she could see her hand tremble as she reached for the small towel. Laila sat behind her, watching silently and sipping tea from a murky glass. As Iris finished splashing her face, Laila extended another glass in her direction, a thumb splayed inside the liquid.

"Where is Lilavati?" Iris asked.

"*Bahar gayee hai.*"

So Lilavati had left the house. Iris quickly glanced around the room. "Maitri… *bahar gayee hai?*"

Laila nodded. Then she thrust the freshly washed jeans and T-shirt into Iris' hand, shoved her lightly and said, "*Chalo bhi!*"

*

Last night, Laila had been instructed by Lilavati to make sure that Iris reached the gates of the right orphanage. Then she was to make herself scarce, leaving Iris on her own. Iris had protested that this would never work, but now she watched with silent respect as Laila proved she was very street-smart for someone so young. She found an auto-rickshaw and barked her orders at the driver, pushing Iris into the vehicle before her. But during the ride in the auto rickshaw Laila sat far away from Iris, making it clear that she wasn't ready to be friends.

Iris watched the rolling meter, placed where a side view mirror should have been, worrying at the rate her money was being spent. She needed to have enough for another trip to an internet café.

Finally, the auto rickshaw stopped. She took out a one hundred rupee note and looked for Laila. The girl was walking away, not looking back. Iris could feel the damp sweat on her back where she had rested against the plastic seat. She raised her right hand to subtly sniff at her underarms and was relieved to smell lemon detergent and sandalwood soap. She straightened her money-belt and took her first step towards the gate, wishing she had sturdier shoes on in case she needed to make a fast getaway.

The two orphanage guards were feasting on watermelon chunks, which they broke off in large gashes from a fruit on a low table. They were too busy catching the slithery drops on the tips of their tongues and wiping off the dribbles on shirtsleeves to notice her approach. Iris cleared her throat. The older guard stood up and did a quick salaam, then he unlatched the gate. Iris couldn't believe it. This was it? The Twin Evils? She could just walk through, no questions asked?

She forced herself not to look back nervously as she walked past the shady arbour and came to the building.

Right in front, under a wide portico, an empty child's crib was prominently displayed. It was a *jhoola*, and Iris' slight touch set it gently swinging to and fro. This must have been where Aman had left the baby. Iris opened the door. The Madam was sitting exactly as Aman had described to Lilavati, except she wore a high-collared blouse in navy blue today. Iris squared her shoulders as the Madam looked her over from the top of her head to her unvarnished toes in the Kolhapuri sandals. Then, just as the silence was starting to grow uncomfortable, the Madam stood up and extended a hand in welcome. "Can I help you? I am Shabnam, and I run this orphanage."

Iris introduced herself and sat down. "I hope you can help me – I…well, we, have come all the way from Ohio." She finished with a nervous giggle.

Shabnam rang the bell. As a maid entered, Shabnam asked Iris, "Will you take something hot or cold?"

"Cold water would be great. Thanks."

Shabnam spoke to the maid in Hindi. She opened a drawer and took out a notebook. "You were saying?"

"We want to adopt a baby girl. Buddhist, Muslim, Hindu, it doesn't matter, but my husband and I want a little girl, not too old…" Iris stopped, realising that she was babbling.

Shabnam looked up from taking notes. "Your husband is here, Mrs… er… Sen? It is unusual for only half the couple to come, but perhaps your husband is otherwise engaged?"

Lilavati had tutored her on this. "He is with his uncle's family; the uncle passed away recently and they are at Benares, immersing the ashes. All these Hindu rituals, you know? I don't believe in all that chanting and feeding, but sometimes you have to do all this." Iris laughed while she wiped her sweaty palms on her jeans.

"Yes."

"He wanted to be here, but I had to come to you first... actually, we are a bit desperate. My mother-in-law is not well and that is why we had to fly in from Ohio. She is in a nursing home in Calcutta now, the last stage of cancer. We want to show her the baby. We want the baby to have her name... so we want a baby before she goes, which could be anytime now."

Iris took a few deep breaths, trying to recall the minutiae of the details she had rehearsed with Lilavati. She gulped nervously. Shabnam stopped rocking back and forth in her chair as her eyes narrowed, "Yes. But is this also important to *you*, Mrs Sen?"

Iris quickly looked down at the floor, trying to force some grief. "She has only sons, my mother-in-law. When I was married... as a new bride... I became her daughter. But I can't have any children... we are very close and nothing would make her happier than to see her own granddaughter, her own flesh-and-blood, you know?"

Shabnam smiled. Iris felt bolder. "This may seem to be playing with the truth, but if a lie makes a dying woman happy, we will do it. We hope to pass off this child as her own blood. My husband has told her that I am still in America but will be arriving soon with the baby. A newborn baby, or a very young one... we are looking everywhere, at all the orphanages. A little girl, possibly one that looks like us... we have tried in Calcutta already, but now we are also searching here, close to Benares while we are here."

Shabnam looked at Iris closely, "And both you and your husband are Bengali? But you live in America?"

"Yes. We are willing to pay whatever it takes to make this happen for my mother-in-law... before it is too late. The doctors are not giving her much time. We want to settle this in a week if possible."

Shabnam's face had an apologetic smile. "A week, Mrs Sen? That is impossible! Even the paperwork..."

Iris squared her shoulders and sat up straighter. She could hear Lilavati's booming voice in her head, "*You* tell *her* what to do!"

"Please call me Iris. Shabnam. Let me be clear about this; my husband has grown up in India even if I haven't, and he understands exactly how things work here. It is unfortunate he can't be here today, but when we were at two orphanages yesterday, we were told that things are possible if we are willing to pay. Those orphanages were going to give us older children almost immediately – we are searching specifically for a newborn girl. We will be here for another week for the rituals, then we would like to return to Calcutta with a baby. I think we should understand each other perfectly so that we don't waste each other's time."

Shabnam played with the pen. "Yes, but er, Iris, you are young, there are some age restrictions... how old are you?"

Iris added five years to her own age and to Danesh. "I am twenty-eight and Danesh is thirty-one."

"You are very young." There was a pause, and Iris felt her heart thudding as Shabnam searched her face. "If you have your own child sometime, that will complicate things."

Iris leaned on the table, pulling her chair closer. "I cannot ever have my own child. That has been proven to be a medical impossibility. We would have tried surrogacy, but we do not have time. This baby will be named after my mother-in-law and she will be a last miracle for my mother-in-law and a gift for us. There is no way that someone so precious will be unloved in our home and we are prepared to pay whatever it takes to get her home before my mother-in-law is gone."

"But never mind," Iris pushed her chair back. "If you cannot help us, I will not waste your time." She stood up. Iris could see Shabnam assessing her closely but she had practiced too hard with Lilavati to drop her gaze.

Shabnam got up hurriedly. "No, no, please sit down. You are simply getting angry for no reason. I have a newborn, a girl, but I need to make sure that she will go to a good home. They are all my children and I have a mother's heart, you understand?"

Iris sat back and allowed herself a brief smile. She had time to gulp down one sip of the cold water before an ayah came into the room. She was in a white sari with the faintest of green borders and holding a tiny bundle. The baby was swaddled in white, her face completely hidden in the folds.

"We named her Piya, but you can change it to give her your mother-in-law's name," Shabnam whispered. "She just fell asleep after a feed."

"Piya, the Beloved. How beautiful! I have a cousin with the same name." Iris reached out gingerly to touch the soft hair, "How old is she?"

"Ten days. Her mother died – labour complications. The father thinks the child is evil, you know, swallowing up the mother's life as soon as she was born. Very sad."

"I see." Iris took out Maitri's cellphone and took two pictures successively, one a close-up.

"No pictures, please," Shabnam snapped.

"For my husband. The baby is so beautiful!" She hit *Send* to the first person on the contact list before Shabnam could object. Maitri had changed the cellphone language to English last night so that Iris would not fumble.

*

The baby was placed on Iris's lap. Iris stroked a smooth cheek and marvelled at the perfection of this little being. She glowed from within; even her tiny mouth glistened with light. How could anyone give up a baby so incandescent? Lilavati was right; Aman had shit for brains. Iris gently hugged Piya and the baby squirmed, finding a new position of comfort. *Like water flowing into a bottle*, thought Iris. *I could get used to this.*

Iris looked up at Shabnam. "I need to talk to my husband of course, but there is no doubt that we will want her." She lowered her voice slightly, "Can we talk about costs?"

Shabnam waved the ayah out of the room as she swung gently in the chair, the tip of her foot touching the ground in short taps. When the door clicked shut, she leaned forward. "Usually it is $35,000, in American currency. But you have come to us directly, without a broker, so we will also have to find the lawyers and the brokers. I think $45,000 is a reasonable amount."

Iris gasped, "Surely, if there is no broker, it should be cheaper? There is no need to pay a middleman…"

Shabnam's smile disappeared. "We are not haggling over *brinjals* in the market, Madam. A broker makes things easier for us – when someone walks in the door like you and expects instant service we have to pay more people. Much more, not less."

Iris looked at the baby again and checked her surge of anger. This baby was worth less than a year's college tuition. Much less than what her volcano-red McLaren, fully loaded, had cost Daddy. She pursed her lips. *Daddy will do this for me.*

"All right. Tell me how to have the money sent to you." There was a slight movement in the window behind the Madam and Iris could see the edges of two bright yellow bobbles holding up two ponytails – Laila.

Iris tried to manoeuvre the baby discreetly, so that her face was towards the window. She resisted the urge to look up again, in case Shabnam followed her gaze. Shabnam was busy filling in a sheet of paper. Iris craned her neck over the table, bringing Piya's face further up and towards the window. Piya gave a soft hiccup and then a low cry.

"There are many ways to transfer the money to us, but we cannot start the process until it is fully paid."

Piya was now softly whimpering, so Iris got up to start pacing with the baby. "Fully paid? Can we split up the payment into four instalments or something? It's a lot of money!" She was by the window now, rocking Piya.

"No. Please understand that quite a bit of this money will be paid under the table. When it is demanded, it must be available."

Iris could see Laila, crouched in the shrubbery, looking straight at the baby. "OK," said Iris. "I will contact my fa – um, the family banker… right away and see about some transfers. After 9/11, any kind of a foreign money transfer needs a lot of form-filling in the States. It may take time."

"I am sure you will handle it, Iris." Shabnam's eyes were unflinching, "full payment, then the baby."

Iris walked back to the edge of the table and stood facing Shabnam. "How long will it take to get the baby once the money has been transferred?"

Shabnam took Piya from Iris' arms in a practiced motion. "One week. Only for you, under such exceptional circumstances, but I guarantee it."

*

When Iris left the orphanage, she didn't know where to look for Laila. The guard stood up and *salaamed* her again, and now he was watching with disinterest as she waited for an empty auto rickshaw to pass. She strolled along the length of the road, discreetly looking into the shrubbery of the orphanage for Laila. She would drop the little girl safely home and go to an internet café before going back to Maitri.

An empty auto rickshaw passed and she shouted. The driver careened to a stop, raising a plume of dust. Where was Laila? Should she just leave? Iris gnawed at her thumb and searched for the piece of paper with Maitri's address scribbled in Hindi and English. What was she supposed to do now; if she left, wouldn't Laila become another lost child? Or was Laila on her way home alone? Iris felt her head throbbing dully.

The driver started the engine and slowed to a crawl as he turned the corner, shaking his head at the piece of paper Iris extended towards him. He couldn't read. Iris looked above his head and saw a little figure at the bus stop, two yellow bobbles on her head, scanning the road. "Stop!" she shouted.

Laila squirmed under the metal partition and into the vehicle, imperiously telling the driver where to go. As the auto rickshaw started again, Iris reached out for the little hand and felt the fingers creep up her palm, lacing through her fingers in quiet collusion. By the time Iris showed Laila the pictures on the cellphone, the little girl was grinning.

Chapter 13

Danesh had woken from an uneven sleep although his room at Hotel Shambala International was very luxurious. Yesterday he had spent a fruitless evening at the railway station trying to find Aman the doll-seller, son of the Tragedy Queen of Bollywood. He felt he was in the middle of a particularly bad episode of the *Twilight Zone*. Everyone knew the son of the Tragedy Queen and Danesh knew the quote about feet on the ground was coming just by hearing the first sound. Yet no one knew where this man lived; his evening had culminated with a visit to another Aman who lived forty kilometres away (he had to pay heavily to get an interpreter to take him there) where a toothless crone had offered him a cool rose-flavoured drink and assured him (through the interpreter) that she had never been a Tragedy Queen anywhere. No one there had heard of any Iris Sen, *was this some Anglo-Indian girl from Kolkata?*

Danesh felt exhausted. There was still no message from Iris although he had his laptop permanently connected to the internet in case she logged on. He scarfed down a quick breakfast of cereal and milk, ignoring the fragrant heaps of *puri* and *alu* in the Indian section of the breakfast buffet, then ran back up to the room to check for messages again. His parents had called twice already and nagged him about finding Iris quickly. His father was trying to trace Dr Sen in whichever Himalayan retreat he was in; Danesh already knew how *that* conversation would go. Everyone was acting as if Iris was two years old and Danesh had managed to lose a toddler in his charge instead of a twenty-three year woman who had graduated from college.

He clicked on the open tabs on his computer half-heartedly. Was this going to be the rest of his life… Iris acting impetuously and irrationally and he being held responsible for her actions? As he had explained to his parents, the chances of Iris being kidnapped were very slight; no one was asking for ransom, he had a message that she was OK, and he also had numerous testimonies about Iris drinking *chai* on the platform and generally loitering around the shops just before the train left. One person claimed to have seen Iris run after the train very slowly, but that Danesh found hard to believe. He gloomily put on his shoes again and headed downstairs. The thought of bumping into Kiku raised his spirits.

*

She was sitting in the marble foyer, framed by a large Buddhist tanka, which Danesh recognised as Tibetan. The green brocaded borders contained the entire universe as the painting rose from a lotus pedestal into a wheel of life. There was the dense blue of the sky above and the darker earth below and miniature Buddhist icons on either side. The red silk flaps fluttered in the icy blast from the air-conditioner and lightly played on her blue-black hair. Kiku looked up from her guidebook and smiled. Danesh felt a jolt of happiness; had she been hoping to see him too?

"So you found this hotel! Did you find your friend?"

Danesh shook his head. "You found the luggage?"

"Yes." Kiku made a face and mimicked the Station Master's tone, "We are the Indian Railways!"

Danesh grinned. "I need to go back to the railway station for leads but I'm keeping far away from that idiot. And you? More sightseeing today?"

She indicated the book in her hand. "Narayan is taking us to Shambalasisa, where the Buddha preached the Fire Sermon."

"Oh? I don't think I've heard of it."

Kiku sighed. "Me neither." She whispered conspiratorially, "I am so bored by this religious tourism."

"Aha. The lady needs some rescuing?"

Kiku cocked her head slightly. "Perhaps."

"Well this knight is headed for Shambala Junction right now. You could run out the front door with me and no one will ever find you."

Kiku wound a lock of long hair around her finger as she considered the idea. "Good. Narayan is driving me nuts with his concern about my *bowel movements*. Give me a second and I will tell my parents I won't be joining them."

Danesh looked at her departing back and thought, *she knows Iris is my fiancée, right?* I haven't lied about anything. He couldn't remember whether he had told her or not, but it seemed an irrelevant detail right now. It wasn't as if he had asked her out on a date. Kiku was an attractive and intelligent woman, and seeing her so early in his morning made him feel that everything would turn out all right in his nightmare-vacation world. He wanted her company badly.

*

It didn't take them long to reach the railway station or to find the interpreter Danesh had used yesterday evening. In fact, the interpreter seemed to be waiting for him; he was a young man, possibly just out of his teens, and he stood out like a neon light in his shiny green polyester shirt and tight black pants. His oversized aviator sunglasses did nothing to deflect his shimmer. After agreeing on three times what Danesh had paid yesterday, they engaged him for the whole day and were on their way, asking around the station again for Aman, married to Maitri. Danesh noticed that people were nicer to him, maybe because he had a woman by his side, or because Kiku was so charming – he really couldn't tell. She was dainty in a porcelain doll sort of way but was sharp enough to ask the right questions when Danesh's frustration overrode his communication skills. Before an hour was up, the interpreter was already turning to her for instructions.

"You are very good with people," Danesh commented after watching Kiku coax an address out of an old woman selling newspapers in a corner. The interpreter beamed with delight while scribbling some numbers on the palm of his hand, followed by the curlicues of an Indic alphabet. Danesh refused to get too excited; following all the red herrings last night had been exhausting. Not to mention expensive.

"Why do these people tell you things while glaring at me?"

"It's on-the-job training. Nothing to it."

Danesh regarded her appraisingly. "Are you, like, some sort of Japanese Oprah? No, wait, didn't you say you live in Amsterdam?"

Kiku burst out laughing, her voice pealing gaily in his ears. He captured this moment in a mental snapshot, *Click*.

"Nothing as glamorous as a talk-show host! Yes, I live in Holland now, but not Amsterdam, it's a tiny city called Leiden where I'm a graduate student. Before that I grew up around the world, went to school in six countries... talking in gestures is my mother tongue!"

"Six countries...! And your research is on what again?"

Kiku stopped and turned to him. The interpreter, who was leading the way, also stopped and looked back at them, puzzled.

"I'm looking at mathematical patterns in Indian folk music so I will go into villages and check out the performances. To analyse evolution and change, that sort of thing," her face softened. "Non-verbal communication has become a necessity, you know, with all the music I study, especially with so many dialects and languages going on in this country."

They walked along the edge of the railway track where it dipped into a slope. The interpreter indicated that they should cross the tracks, with a hasty glance in either direction.

"Seriously? He wants us to cross the train track?"

"Oh come on!" Kiku jumped down and trotted after the interpreter. Danesh hurried to keep up.

"I'm afraid I'm totally ignorant about Indian music."

"Oh," Kiku waved her arm dismissively, "It's not important to know much to enjoy the music, is it?"

The guide, who had been nervously watching the multiple rows of parallel tracks, now pushed Danesh's elbow. A train was slowly rounding a corner in the distance. They crossed the tracks hurriedly and climbed into the back of a white Maruti Suzuki waiting outside the gates of the station.

Shambala was full of people; at one point they navigated their way through a narrow bazaar at snail's pace while the fragrance of ripe mangoes wafted in through the open windows of the car. Flies buzzed in the nectared air, sonorous and dazed. Danesh wanted to taste one of those heady fruits but when he turned to Kiku again, she had a thin film of sweat on her upper lip.

"Are you OK?" She nodded. "The cramps are back, but I am all right, thanks." He patted her hand in reassurance and she didn't pull away.

*

When they knocked at the door of a run-down apartment at the end of a bustling block of similar buildings (after three false leads), Danesh was sure they had come to the wrong place again. A retinue of small children followed them through the narrow lane and the interpreter stood at the base of the steps, trying to shoo them away. The door was opened by an old lady who was, clearly, not the Tragedy Queen, for Danesh had been told by many people that the Tragedy Queen had drunk herself to death. This woman, like the one he met yesterday, would surely now tell him that he had the wrong house.

She was not tall, but had a certain rigidity that made her appear formidable, even in a crumpled cotton sari with frayed green edges. The matching green glass bangles clinked gently on her arm as she used the edge of her sari to wipe wheat flour off her hands as she looked Danesh up and down. Then she gave Kiku the same treatment. She looked like a severe schoolteacher who could subdue a raucous class of teenage boys with just her flinty eyes.

Danesh felt certain this hovel must be the wrong house. He couldn't imagine Iris staying five minutes in such a place and he started to back away, but was stopped by the woman's voice.

"What do you want?" the woman asked Kiku in English. Danesh would have been thrilled at her English had her frown not been so belligerent. He stepped further back as Kiku stepped toward the woman.

This was clearly a mistake. Aman the doll-seller was reported to be both illiterate and insane and Danesh felt he knew enough about Indian class structures to know that any English speaker was unlikely to be related.

He could hear Kiku's singsong voice telling his story, and just as he was about to take her arm and pull her into a hurried good bye he heard the woman say, "Iris? She is not here. At orphanage. But will be back soon. Come in. I am Lilavati. Aman's mother-in-law."

Danesh saw Kiku perform a slight bow before stepping over the threshold. He followed her inside, thinking, *Orphanage? They put Iris in an orphanage? Why?* Nothing made sense in this place. He stepped into a gloomy room, with two small windows, and as Lilavati opened the curtains the afternoon light fell on a series of large movie posters. Danesh moved towards the first poster; could this be, finally, The Tragedy Queen? A woman's portrait was painted in stark brush-strokes of orange, red and black paint. The buxom heroine had tears of red blood flowing down her large eyes that were ringed by a line of kohl so dark that she looked like a grieving raccoon. She loomed Amazonian over the smaller pictures of a couple in an embrace and a man looking trenchantly out at the viewer. Danesh indicated the poster as he turned to the interpreter. "Which movie is this?"

Lilavati made an odd noise in her throat. "That's the Tragedy Queen."

The interpreter started to read the text in the semi-gloom, "*Randi ki kothe ki dastaan,*" he said. Then he rolled his eyes, "*The Story of a Prostitute's Brothel… chee,* what dirty language they put on posters, see! But this movie has very romantic dialogues…"

"Yes, yes, I know," Danesh hurriedly interrupted before he too started quoting the dirty feet thing.

"You must be the husband?" asked Lilavati, turning to Danesh.

Kiku raised her eyebrows as Danesh stared at Lilavati. Before he could respond, there was a shriek of excitement as the door burst open and a little girl flew into Lilavati's arms, screeching excitedly in Hindi.

"What happened?" Danesh asked the interpreter.

"She says they found the baby," the interpreter shrugged.

Then, framed in the light of the open door, Danesh saw Iris. Her hair was grimy and dishevelled – was this the same clean-freak Iris? But she was laughing happily while watching Lilavati and the little girl. She still hadn't seen him but she was trying to tie her hair into that familiar loose knot at the nape of her neck. Even dirty, she looked gorgeous. The interpreter stared at her.

Then Iris saw Danesh and froze, arms still raised. With a whoop, she ran into his arms, knocking him off his feet, so that they collapsed into the charpoy behind them. Danesh clasped his arms around her waist in a hug even as he felt Lilavati's displeasure and the interpreter's salacious eyes. The charpoy sagged dangerously as Danesh lifted his neck. Behind Iris' head, he could see Kiku walking out the door.

*

Danesh pushed himself up onto his elbows with some difficulty, struggling against Iris' weight on him. He could still see Kiku through the open door. Some neighbourhood urchin asked her a question and she shook her head vigorously. Iris' voice brought him back.

"Dan! Babe, I'm *so* glad you're here! I was *so* worried about you!"

He was also relieved to see her again and grinned broadly. "Worried about *me*?"

"I know, I know… I shouldn't have got off the train, but how did you find me? Did you get my message?"

He could still summon up his irritation, despite the relief that she was found. "Why did you even get off a train in the middle of the night, *alone*, and not get back on? And why didn't you send me an email to tell me exactly where you were in the past 24 hours? Especially if you are like visiting random orphanages?"

Danesh could feel his head swivelling helplessly back and forth to find Kiku, but he could catch only glimpses through the gaggle of children surrounding her.

"There was some 'load-shedding'" Iris said as she made charming bunny-ears with crooked fingers, "you know, like no power anywhere? I tried…"

Danesh suddenly realised that he couldn't see Kiku anymore. The doorway was still barred by a number of dirty children, all watching them as if it were prime time on the Disney Channel. He half listened as Iris chattered on about a missing baby and Aman. It was too much for Danesh. He rudely interrupted, "OK, get your stuff and let's go. We can talk about this at the hotel."

The interpreter and Lilavati stopped their conversation at his tone. Iris gave a nervous, girlish laugh and reached for his hand again. "I know you're upset," she seemed to be getting ready to snuggle into his shoulder but one look at the children and she changed her mind. She played with his fingers instead and said softly, "It's OK. I'm OK. You've found me now."

She was *managing* him again, soothing him as his temper reached boiling point. To calm himself down, Danesh extracted his fingers and held his head in his hands. He realised the hypocrisy of that action immediately; to everyone else, it probably looked as if he was exhausted and relieved and that the strain of being away from Iris had been too much for him. But he sat with his eyes closed, wondering if Kiku would find her way out from this place without being molested and whether he would ever see her again. He looked up and addressed the interpreter. "The Japanese lady... please find her. Take her back to the hotel." He shoved some notes into his hands.

Lilavati looked at Iris and then back at Danesh. "She is staying in your hotel? With you?" asked Lilavati.

"Who *was* that?" Iris asked simultaneously.

Danesh ignored Lilavati. "She is visiting Shambala with her parents... she's a Japanese researcher. Her name is Kiku."

"I kind of just saw you and like totally ignored her. I was so glad to see you, you know... I totally didn't notice her," said Iris, unhappily looking at the open door.

"But if she is staying in the same hotel, no problem. You know where to find her," said Lilavati. Now both women were looking at Danesh.

He said irritably, "Yes. There is only one decent hotel in this city."

"What's her name again?"

"Kiku. So let's get your stuff and go now."

140

"Yes, yes, go visit the hotel," urged Lilavati, "Have a nice talk, get your husband's things, but don't forget we have a meeting with Lakshmy Mittal today, hahn? You must come back and if it gets late, you both stay for the night here, with us." She waved an expansive arm that took in the whole room.

Danesh was familiar with exuberant offers of Indian hospitality and the etiquette of declining them. He looked around the room and firmly said, "I think not."

There was a definite chill in the atmosphere. Even the urchins, randomly violent with each other's body parts while jostling at the door, quietened in the silence. Iris put an arm around Lilavati's shoulders.

"I *want* to help them, Danesh, to find the missing baby." She took out a cellphone and scrolled to Piya's picture, "It's a long story... here, this baby... she has been sort of kidnapped and we are trying to get her back before she gets sold... it's a really complicated situation. Want to go get a quick drink somewhere while I fill you in on this and get back here, Dan? We really need to meet with a human rights lawyer today, time's running out for this baby and..." Iris trailed off.

Danesh looked wearily at her. "I'm fucking exhausted," he kissed the top of Iris' head, "I'm done. If you think you need to run after this baby instead of coming back with me... I'm done. I can't force you to go anywhere but I'm going back to Shambala International for a cold beer now. Even if I have to go alone." He felt as if the whole room was holding its breath while he reined in sharper words. Dammit, she knew him better than anyone else, couldn't she see that he wanted her to leave right now?

141

Iris stood immobile. Danesh scrabbled his pocket for his mobile phone and gave it to Iris, "I get it. Call me later. The hotel number's programmed in."

"I'll come later, Dan, OK? After the meeting with Lakshmy... or I can come with you now, for about an hour, then come back here again..."

"I'm not interested in standing here and arguing about your priorities right now."

Lilavati was looking at him as if to ask: *That's it, lover boy?* Iris stood on tiptoe and gently brushed his lips with hers, ignoring the shocked murmur of the watching crowd.

When Danesh left, closing the door shut firmly behind him, Iris could hear soft scratches of the children, like little rodents, milling outside the door. She felt like crying.

"Well," said Lilavati, "Let me see the phone picture."

Her businesslike tone, coupled with a glass of hot tea, helped lighten the mood. As Lilavati peered at the grainy pictures, both showing the same unsmiling face, Laila laughed out loud and hugged Lilavati. But Lilavati said something sharply in Hindi. She waved the cellphone in the air. "I am telling you both now, this doesn't prove *anything*. You tried, but this is a very bad picture, it looks like the melon-seller's newborn son, who can tell?"

Laila said something to her grandmother, quick and angry, but Lilavati shushed her. "We need a plan," Lilavati sighed heavily, "like father, like daughter. This family has no brains. We have to think of something."

"Can't we get the police to raid this orphanage based on Laila's testimony and this picture of the child? I can also tell them about Shabnam and how much I was quoted for this child…"

The fury in Lilavati's eyes made Iris stop. "Do you think, Iris, that the police don't know of this ring? Is it possible for babies to be bought and sold like this without fake certificates and payments? You have no proof at all – and Madam was very careful not to give you any copies of the forms, no? This Madam is very smart and well connected; our proof has to be stronger than her money."

"Can we talk to the newspapers? Maybe a TV channel?" Iris ventured.

Lilavati picked up the yellowing newspaper used to line the storage area under the bed. "Look at the headlines, 'Child bitten by dog and dies in slum', 'Five schoolchildren die in school bus accident'… until this baby is dead, no journalist will touch this story!"

Iris turned away in shock; this was her granddaughter's murder that Lilavati was talking about. Lilavati sucked at her teeth noisily, thinking. "No one can do anything," she pronounced carefully, "except for Lakshmy Mittal. You did as much as you could today, thank you, but we need the Tigress. Maitri is teaching at the Buddhist School today… she will come later and meet us. Come with me."

Chapter 14

When the auto rickshaw stopped in front of the house, its distinctive *phut-phut-phut* revving to a last *phruut* and dying away, Lakshmy Mittal knew that Lilavati had come. And she wondered again why she had offered to help. This should have been a restful evening after a particularly gruelling week at the Allahabad High Court.

Lakshmy twitched the curtains aside. A young girl, clearly a Non Resident Indian by the way she carried herself, was stepping out; she could see a pair of dusty Kolhapuri sandals and jean-clad legs emerging from the rickshaw. The girl was sweltering – the dark blue of the jeans and her tight T-shirt were sticking to her body. But beyond it all, she could see the girl's outlined youth.

Lakshmy turned away from the mirror in the hallway. Lilavati had not mentioned bringing an NRI when they had spoken on the phone. Dealing with NRIs was unbearably tedious. Most were self-righteous do-gooders whose notion of community service was to spend a few hours visiting villages so they could donate their dollars in person. The young ones were the most difficult, especially when focused on completing the Creativity, Action and Service quota in their IB prep schools to get into Ivy League colleges... and they rarely spoke any language that would connect them to the communities they wanted to serve.

Lakshmy had dealt with too many young women of this type. Groups of them spent summers at her organisation until about two years ago, when she started saying 'No'. Prakash, her husband, had studied at the hallowed halls of the Indian Institute of Technology and was enmeshed in the notoriously large global network; she had no doubt that the fathers of the girls sat and Googled *charity* and *India* and *human rights* or some such combination, found her name, and linked her to Prakash. And Prakash said 'Yes', indiscriminately. 'Yes' to overseas jobs that were challenging but took him away for years on end (he was now in Dubai); 'Yes' to his extended family members who couldn't seem to get daughters married without his money, 'Yes' to Lakshmy working at a job that brought more death threats than money. Prakash was the solid engineering type who made the best of what life dealt him. He had no idea of what made Lakshmy tick. No idea of what fanned her blood with desire in middle age.

Lakshmy would not think of all that now. The two women outside were arguing with the auto-rickshaw driver, or rather, Lilavati was. She wouldn't have to open the door just yet, so she turned and caught her reflection in the mirror again.

The doorbell rang. Lilavati stood with the girl on her doorstep. Lakshmy took in a slight sour smell and opened the door wider to fan the odour out of her nose.

"Please come in." She could see the girl hesitate at the door, unsure of whether to be the first to enter.

"This heat has been so difficult this year, I hope the cold arrives soon…" Lilavati marched in, familiar with her surroundings, and her voice disappeared into a room.

Lakshmy turned to watch the girl shutting the door behind her, and blinking in the sudden gloom of the hallway. The house was cool and clean and gleamed softly with marble and glass and granite. It had corners with splashes of colour and backlit statues posing artistically, but the overall impression was of reticent wealth, as understated as the antique carpets laid on the floor for dusty feet to walk on. Lakshmy hoped the NRI would have the decency to take off her filthy sandals.

*

There was a swing in the middle of the sitting room on which Lakshmy preferred to sit, gently swinging. Now, she fingered the metal peacocks on the chain as she read through a file. Her mind wandered as Lilavati made the introductions:

> *I will be your Caffe Corretto*
> *foreign, with bitter dregs*
> *the whiff of sambuca*
> *unfiltered, from a spiced bazaar*
> *ravishing the wary tongue;*

Lakshmy shook her head to get the poet's whisper out of her brain and tried to pay attention to Lilavati again.

So this NRI was named Iris. She registered the way the girl swept her palms over her jeans, as if wiping away grime from her hands. The girl was distracted by her mobile phone, toying with it while listening to Lilavati with half her attention. All these brats, thought Lakshmy, glued to their devices only. This generation of women completely lacked focus and this girl, Iris, seemed a prime example. Lakshmy turned her attention back to Lilavati.

"This is the file on the orphanage… Anath Aashray. They seem to be clean. Either that, or they have not been caught yet. But they do deal with Vidyut, that American child-trafficker… he hasn't been charged in the courts yet."

"Is there any hope? The child has been missing for two days now!"

Lakshmy turned the metal chain as she mentally counted the number of such missing-children cases she had handled. "The earlier we know about these cases, the better our chances… two days is already a long time." A look at Lilavati's face and Lakshmy softened her tone, "but it's not too late, we can still find her."

Lakshmy slid off the wide wooden seat and opened the door of the Kashmiri cabinet with ornate *chinar* leaves carved into walnut wood. She took out two folders and laid them out on the coffee table, covering an illustrated book of Ghalib's poetry.

*

Iris picked up another samosa from the plate in front of her and bit into it. The two huddled women were paying no attention to her and she hoped they would be finished soon. She needed to call Danesh back. Although she had whispered into the mobile when he had called, a frown from Lilavati forced her to disconnect that call.

The cook came in with freshly fried *hing kachoris*. Lakshmy and Lilavati ignored the food as they sorted through a large pile of papers. There was a large framed collage of newspaper articles on the wall, the largest of which stated, "Victory for child-rights activist Lakshmy Mittal!" Iris rose, wiping each finger delicately on a napkin to get rid of the samosa grease. She moved closer to read them.

"Ah, New Yorkers – that woman just won't give up!" Lakshmy stood at her shoulder and pointed to the collage. "Do you know about the Chaya case?"

"I was just reading about it."

"I'll summarise it for you. A freelance journalist showed up to do a story on Indian orphanages and came across Chaya. She says it was love at first sight for her, but Chaya had already been chosen by an Indian couple who were going through the adoption process. So this journalist and her husband made a quality-of-life judgement-that you Americans seem to be so fond of making – and decided that Chaya would be better off with them."

Iris looked at her coolly while Lakshmy continued, "They managed to pull all kinds of strings and get the necessary approvals for adoption. Chaya was due to leave India in two months when the Indian parents came to us, quite desperate. No one else was listening to their story."

"Lilavati said you run an organisation of some sort?"

Lilavati looked up from a large black file she was holding in her lap and chided, "Oho, not any 'organisation of some sort'! Lakshmy fights for children... for child rights ... she is a very very famous lawyer. She brings in the destitute girls the Buddhist nuns have in the shelter – the ones Maitri and I teach. She had to move every court until the Supreme Court to prove that the foreign adoption system in India is corrupt and encourages trafficking in children, especially in the Chaya case," she beamed at Lakshmy, "but if anyone can do it, it is Lakshmy Mittal, our Tigress!"

"*I* don't do anything on my own," Lakshmy said quickly. "It's people like you, and Maitri, and all the other activists, who educate the girls and give them life-skills and teach them to fight for their rights. I just shout very loudly in very public places."

"So some families do sell their girls then?" Iris asked in disbelief.

"The poor ones do, sometimes. We discovered that babies have been sold for as little as US$20 and then the adoptive parents pay as much as $25,000 for the adoption process. Quite a tidy profit for the middleman, even after paying all associated legal costs, eh?"

"I was quoted $35,000 for Piya, just as starting costs."

Lakshmy nodded. "I made some calls after Lilavati called me. There is another woman trying to adopt Piya, a white woman, so you have serious competition. Shabnam will milk you both as much as she can, so expect the quoted costs to go up quickly."

Lakshmy sighed, "This woman is also a journalist."

"So, what happened to Chaya? Is she going to New York?"

Lakshmy shrugged. "Who knows? We have a lot of public opinion on our side, but that American woman still shows up at the orphanage every evening even though neither side is allowed to visit Chaya. Quite a media moment – a blonde foreigner with a chic wide hat shading her from the sun, crying over a photo album outside an orphanage."

She looked at Lilavati. "But your case is different. Your granddaughter is not an orphan and she was not offered for adoption through legal means. We just have to prove her connection to your daughter – Roop? Yes. Perhaps a DNA test will do it, but no judge will order one unless we have some hard evidence. The orphanage will have all the fake birth certificates and the relinquishment forms required for the adoption by now."

Iris' brow furrowed. "What if I adopt her first – like, legally... I'll have to pay the money, right, and then they give me the baby? And then return her to Lilavati and start a police case? We can do the DNA testing while she is with me..."

The look on Lakshmy's face stopped Iris. "If you are here to adopt this baby, I will not help you. There are too many NRIs now getting into the adoption arena and frankly, I am very suspicious of why there is so much interest among people of Indian origin to take as many Indians as possible overseas, especially children who can't decide for themselves."

"I *don't* want to take this baby back with me! But isn't it true that these children have better opportunities with us, in America?"

Lakshmy sneered and looked around her room slowly. "Why? Why would you say that the quality of your life was better than mine?"

The doorbell rang again, cutting through the tension. Lilavati hurried to the window. "Maitri is here!"

"Good, we can finish this quickly then." Lakshmy softened her tone. "Let me tell you something else, Iris… the families in India that want to adopt, well, they have to be of a certain socio-economic class to qualify. To put it crassly, these kids don't get adopted into slums. So if food and shelter is not the issue, the other stuff is just icing on the cake and it makes you sick if you have too much."

Lakshmy's cellphone vibrated on the coffee table. Iris could see *Café Corretto* flashing until Lakshmy hit reject quickly. Then Maitri bustled in with apologies and an expansive smile for everyone. The three women went over their strategy in rapid Hindi, sitting even closer while the files were riffled through. They were so engrossed in their talk that they barely noticed Iris fuming on a chair until she interrupted their conversation.

"Lakshmy, I have a question." Lilavati groaned softly and Maitri looked up, puzzled. Lakshmy looked as if she had completely forgotten Iris was still there. "Yes, *beta*?"

"I still can't believe families are selling their daughters for $20. But if a payment of $20 allows more girls to be born instead of being aborted, and then they go to loving families, what is the problem?"

Lakshmy sighed deeply. "Iris, I assume you are asking this probably because you know that nearly ten million female foetuses have been aborted in this country over the past two decades? Right? But if we start paying women to breed girls just to sell them, what does that say about how women are valued, eh? Or did you mean something else entirely?" Iris was stumped into silence as Lakshmy went on, "Abortion is legal here, as it should be, so who are we to dictate whether a woman can abort? Why should women be treated as imbeciles who need help with deciding who to give birth to – surely, if they are aborting girls, it must be because it *is* harder for them to bring them up."

"That's just unethical."

Lakshmy's eyes glinted with a challenge. "Well don't give me partial solutions like adoptions overseas – it just legalises the commodification of our little girls." Her face softened, "Yes, the abortion of female foetuses is a real problem, in certain states more than others, but the reality is that more boys than girls are given up for adoption now. Probably because if a girl survives the foetal stage, she'll be OK. We've fought hard for new laws that specify that before a child can be adopted by foreigners she must first be offered to an Indian couple; then to an Indian couple living abroad; then to a couple with one Indian spouse." Lakshmy paused. "Although there is a hierarchy of qualifications, it still comes down to the highest bidder, and that means rich foreign couples. We have managed to stop these adoptions in Andhra Pradesh, but I would like to see a nationwide moratorium for some years. The traffickers need to be put out of business first."

Lilavati chimed in, "Nobody *I* know would sell her baby," she assured Iris, "and even that idiot my Roop married, lost the child for free. It's not in every alley and home that we are selling our children."

Maitri changed the subject quickly. "Lakshmyji, what is happening with your Chaya case? Dragging on for two years now and the child is still in the orphanage? I hear that letters from US politicians are coming in to sway the judges... is that true?"

Lakshmy sighed, "I don't know what to believe except that this journalist has remarkable faith in the superpowers of her passport – imagine if I were to try to adopt a Caucasian child from Ohio by sheer bullying! But that is what is happening."

"Was Chaya sold by her parents?" asked Iris.

"No, she was abandoned at an orphanage. Orphanages here are sometimes fairly lax about how they receive children."

Lilavati made a face. "Roop didn't marry the only fool in town, we have too many people who think girls are disposable."

Iris felt that she was learning more about the real world here today than during all her years at college in America. She'd always accepted the status quo, unquestioningly. *But the men in her life were different, weren't they?* They only wanted her to be happy.

*

Lakshmy was taking notes; copious scrawls filled page after page of the blue-lined pages of a hardcover notebook with a shiny red spine. The maid came in with another steaming teapot. Iris was surprised to see the sky had darkened outside.

Her phone vibrated in her pocket again, then stopped abruptly. Almost certainly Danesh. Iris briefly wondered whether to call him back now; he had called three hours earlier, and she hadn't found the time to call him back since then. The first thing she would do when they stepped out of Lakshmy's house would be to call him to tell him that she was on her way to see him right now. She also needed to ask whether Danesh had found her parents. She would just wait, it couldn't be much longer.

Lakshmy flexed her fingers. "I first have to find out whether this orphanage is linked to any of the other rogue adoption agencies on our list. I have been informed that LifeSavers India is connected but we have to prove it." She shook her head, "That Vidyut Kapoor is something else – he genuinely believes he can zoom down in an airplane to rescue all our children. It's difficult to deal with someone so misguided, but I have taken him on before and won."

Iris focused on a newspaper clip on the table and tried to remember whether she had heard Vidyut Kapoor's name before. Lakshmy made her feel so stupid that she was intimidated into silence. She was also exhausted and anxious about Danesh. Yet Lakshmy kept droning on. Iris tried to swallow her resentment and brushed off a few *kachori* crumbs from her jeans.

"What's our plan?" asked Lilavati.

"I've sent some people to make inquiries about Anath Aashray but apparently the child is now at the Wings of An Angel Home again; let's see what they find there. Nothing happens in this city without someone seeing something. We just have to find the right people. I'll need to talk to your son-in-law and the family immediately. Let me get some international child-rights activists involved; we may need them if this develops into another Chaya case."

"Can the Buddhist School help? We can form a group to be at the orphanage as soon as in an hour," Maitri offered.

"Have them on standby, but we don't want to do anything to warn off the orphanage in advance... It will take some time to get to your home Lilavati, I need to call some people in the government agencies. Tomorrow's a holiday also, so it may be difficult."

She caught Iris' eye. "Iris, beta, please don't take offence at what I said earlier. I'm just very impatient with short-term solutions. I need you here as well, OK? The police will need a statement about your being offered this baby for sale."

The phone buzzed again and Iris dropped it while fumbling to get it out of her pocket. "Hello? Hello Danesh? Hello?"

The voice was strident, "This is Uncle Sen... Danesh?"

Her father's voice wiped out all other thoughts from Iris' mind. She sniffed loudly, reigning in her surging emotions. There was the familiar slurring of his words, his anxiety tinged with relief, saying "Hello, *ke, ma lokkhi?*" and at that childhood nickname, Iris just sniffed harder, feeling totally choked.

Chapter 15

The sun was dipping into the horizon of the grimy day when Vidyut faced Shabnam across the wide expanse of a table strewn with papers, with Iris' and Emily's applications on top. Shabnam tapped a sheaf gently with her pencil. "This Indian girl will pay at least ten thousand dollars over the market price. We can get more, I'm sure."

Vidyut's eyes narrowed. "I have brought Emily all the way from America for this baby. I am telling you, it will be impossible to explain a change of plans."

Shabnam's right hand swatted at the air gently, "This baby, that baby, what's the difference? I will find a replacement baby for Emily in two days, I guarantee it."

Vidyut looked away as he sipped beer from a dark bottle. The Flying Horse beer was well-chilled, just as he liked it.

"You don't understand, Shabnam. Emily will give this girl a good home. She and her family, I met her father also, I saw with my own eyes how happy they will make any baby they get. This Indian girl, I don't know… she just doesn't sound right."

Shabnam rocked back on her chair, toeing the ground like an impatient horse. "I need to get this baby off my hands fast and out of the country. Between the redhead and this NRI, the young Indian will be much faster to process, you know that. You should have heard her talk, the way she sat… she is obviously a sentimental fool and rich too."

Vidyut shook his head. "You don't want to lose Emily's business over this child! Emily wants to see the baby again, as soon as possible. I have not been taking all her calls, but I have to see her now to convince her that all's OK. She is very nervous about this."

"She saw the baby yesterday!"

"Emily is totally serious about bonding with this baby and taking her home." He paused and continued, "You know how these *firangs* can get, all emotional like that only… I'm still not convinced about this NRI you want to give the baby to."

Shabnam's face was benign as she spoke in formal Hindi, "I would take offence at this Vidyut, but you are like a younger brother to me. I am amazed at how you come from overseas, fly in for ten days and think that you can teach me how to run my business here. I have seen many like you come and go, while I have been here," she agitated a pencil between her the tips of her fingers, "for twenty-seven years."

He could see she knew he would detect the rebuke under her words and wouldn't take it lightly. Vidyut sighed in resignation. Her reference to him as a younger brother had made him aware of other obligations. He was supposed to go to Meerut to meet his elder sister tomorrow evening – a sister he hadn't seen for two years. He did not want to linger in Shambala and investigate some random Indian woman from America. "Fine," he said curtly, "I have never had any reason to doubt your judgement, it's a bad gut feeling only. But I want a new baby girl here in two days, when I return from Delhi."

He smiled slightly, "Emily's fallen in love with this *bacchi*. Can you arrange for a look-alike?"

Shabnam was still chuckling when Vidyut's phone rang. She looked up in concern as he said a few terse words into the mouthpiece and hung up.

"Lakshmy Mittal," he said with emphasis, "has been asking about my connection to Anath Aashray."

Shabnam leaned forward, her brow furrowed, "Does she know about Emily?"

"Yes. She also knows the baby's name…"

"My people have not called me…"

"Maybe I pay mine better. How the fuck would I know? This was a call from someone who works with Mittal. The bitch is sniffing hard."

Shabnam pursed her lips, then leaned back. "It's hard to wave thirty-five thousand dollars good bye. But I should have known this would happen when the baby's father created so much trouble outside the orphanage… that Mittal would be called to pick up this case…"

"Never mind Mittal!! What are *we* doing about the baby?"

Shabnam's eyes glinted at Vidyut, who was pacing up and down the room. "We'll just have to make this baby disappear very quickly. I'll move her tonight."

"And then what? What do I tell Emily when I see her now? What are you telling the Indian woman?"

"I am handling this. Everything will be fine in two days. Nothing we haven't come up against before." Shabnam waved a dismissive hand, "Go, go now. You go handle your Emily-Shemily and let me handle my business."

*

An hour later, Vidyut wove his way through the maze of tables at Shambala International and found Emily absentmindedly chewing on the end of a pen. A large extended family of at least four generations was celebrating a birthday noisily in a corner. The remains of her half-eaten dinner congealed on the plate as Emily scribbled something on saffron cardstock decorated with peacocks and Indian dancers. There was a big sticker of baby Krishna at the centre, his divine mouth open, showing a vision of the stars and the universe.

"Sorry to barge in on your dinner," Vidyut said cheerily. She beamed at him. "Thanks for coming, Vee." She put the card away, "I was just writing a note to my niece."

He pulled up a chair, "All OK? You sounded kind of worried on the phone…"

"Oh, I'm OK. I've been trying to call you about seeing the baby again."

He waved his cellphone in the air. "I know, I know… I needed to recharge my SIM card, but this is such a small backward place, everything is complicated, sorry!" Seeing her nod, Vidyut continued, "I've been trying to get a meeting with Piya set up but things work *really slowly* in India!"

"Yeah, I know." Emily smiled, "So I decided to help you. I got the phone number of the orphanage. It was on the board outside the main doors. When I called, they said, if you saw her yesterday, you have to wait three to four days to see her again." She paused, "I don't want to hear that kind of crap, Vee."

"I can't do anything more than what I've been doing Emily. I can't *force* them, y'know…"

"Well, that's not good enough. That woman we met said I could see her whenever… I want you to come with me tomorrow, and I want to see her again."

The silence lengthened. The sound of a glass breaking was followed by the squeals of a child, followed by shouts. They both swivelled their heads to see a waiter dabbing at a spreading stain on the carpet while another dabbed politely and ineffectually in the direction of an outraged child, who was bawling openly. Vidyut's voice was apologetic. "I have to be in Meerut tomorrow evening. Look, Emily, I return in two days, and then we'll see the baby. Shabnam has promised me…"

"Look Vee, let's get this straight, I haven't come to another country just to sit in an empty hotel room for days waiting to see my baby."

Vidyut turned to signal the waiter, buying some time while he ordered a drink. "Emily, give me a break here!

Tomorrow's a holiday and most places are gonna be closed anyways. I hear you, but I can't force these people to work on holidays, can I?"

Emily did not smile back. "This just doesn't feel right, Vee. I have also been commissioned to write about the whole adoption process in India. I can't just sit on my hands waiting for things to happen."

He flailed desperately, reading the threat implicit in her words. "I've been in this business for twelve years, Emily. There's nothing to worry about. Believe me…"

She flicked the pen down. "Don't patronize me, Vee. I want to talk to that woman now, the one in charge, that Shambam whatshername?"

"Shabnam." He breathed a sigh of relief. What a good idea – Shabnam was the best at handling a crisis of the parental kind. She would talk to Emily and reassure her that all was well, and he, Vidyut, would be home free. Otherwise, this nutcase wannabe mummy would jabber on about needing to bond with the baby. Taking the cellphone out of his pocket, he speed-dialled Shabnam and handed Emily the phone. He looked around the restaurant as they both waited for the network to connect.

The couple on his right, an Indian man and a Japanese woman, were so engrossed in each other that they didn't look away from each other once, not even as a birthday party group let out a stream of whoops and shrill whistles.

"Hello, Shabnam? This is Emily. Fine, thanks. Can I ask you a quick question? Thanks. Why has Piya been moved from the orphanage I saw her in?"

Vidyut turned his head sharply to look at Emily.

"Yes," she said, deliberately enunciating each syllable. "I am sure. I paid the hotel driver to go on his own and ask about where she is. He had to bribe some people to find out, but I know that she is at some..." she checked the notations in a small notebook, "*An-ath Ash-ray.*" Her voice dripped venom. "Does Vee even know about this? Here, why don't you ask him?"

The phone sounded the beeps of a disconnected call as she handed it back to him and leaned back. Her eyes assessed him as he calculated his next move.

"Did you *really* think that I would just sit around this fancy hotel and wait for you to call me, Vee? Especially when you haven't been taking my calls the whole day? I'm a trained reporter Vee, just remember that. I'm not the average dumbass you deal with. Don't even try to mess with me."

Her eyes were shards of green. "Don't even, for a moment, think that I'm going to leave India without this baby in my arms after all I've been through for the past year.

With or without your help, Vee, Piya is coming home with *me*."

Chapter 16

Before their meal, Danesh led Kiku onto the large open balcony with stand fans that whirred out mists of icy cool water, while larger ceiling fans circled overhead. There was a view of the street, teeming with traffic, where a dusky white cow stood placidly in the middle of the mess, one bent hoof signalling her intent to sit down more comfortably. An elderly man rushed out of his small Maruti and nudged the cow gently with a briefcase.

"*Hut, hut,*" he said softly, then more loudly, with folded hands, "*Arre hut meri Ma!*" And the cow turned her head with slow bovine placidity before lifting her tail and depositing a plop of poop.

Kiku laughed out loud. "India's like an open-air circus... I love this drama. If only I could get used to the food!"

The waiter offered them two menus. "How're you feeling now?" Danesh asked.

Kiku wobbled her palm in the air, "So-so. I'll have a cold coffee please."

Danesh looked at the alcohol selection and made a snap decision. "A *kalboishakhi* for me, thanks."

Kiku sniffed the air theatrically and asked, "Hasn't someone had a few already?" and sank back into the flowery yellow and blue cushions.

"Let's just say I need another one."

She shrugged. "Hey, don't let me stop you. Where's Iris?"

Danesh was grateful that she hadn't asked about his fiancée, or said 'your wife'.

"I need to explain about Iris…"

"Not if you don't want to. I assume there's a good reason you didn't tell me you were looking for more than a friend."

"She's my fiancée."

"Ah?" There was a slight pause. "She's very pretty. Do you want to ask her to join us for a drink now?"

"Iris has decided to do a Mother Theresa and will be slumming it with her new family. To rescue a baby or something…" He smiled grimly, "I don't get it. Maybe Aman's insanity is contagious."

"Or she has good reasons for wanting to stay."

He didn't want to tell Kiku about how angry or irrelevant he felt now that Iris was fired up about something else; it would make him sound like a loser.

The silence grew longer as Kiku stretched a lazy hand along her back and adjusted the sunflower patterned cushion behind her. Clearly, she was not going to say anything until he spoke first. He looked at the cool woman in front of him, so self-possessed, so unfazed... so very unlike Iris.

"What do you think I should do?" He asked her as if they were discussing a naughty child.

But that wicked smile hovered around Kiku's lips again. "Are you upset that she doesn't want to come running back to you, or are you upset that she may be in real danger from the criminal elements?"

"She's a spoilt little princess, Kiku. You should see how she lives in Ohio – geez, she's never lived with people like that before!"

"A princess? Really?" Kiku's eyes mocked him even as her voice was even. "Poor thing is now stuck with the plebs, eh?"

"I'm just saying it's not safe out there. Do you know how bad it is for women travelling alone in India nowadays?"

Kiku held out her phone solemnly. "See all these missed calls? That's my Dutch university, threatening to pull my funding unless I return immediately. *Only* because I am a female researcher travelling alone in India. Don't preach."

"Oh God, I had no idea. What are you going to do?"

"Do? I am getting to Kolkata early to get started on my research. You know, as soon as I can change the dates with my interviewees, I am going to get this work done before the administrators have time to pull the plug on it completely."

"I don't know what to say... are you sure?"

"Look Danesh, I have been in countries a lot more dangerous than this one. Iris will be fine. Why don't you tell me what's really bothering you – you didn't really think the old woman or that little girl was a threat, did you?"

He took a deep breath and told her about a childhood betrothal that no one had expected to become real. That this was the most mis-timed adventure ever, especially as his extended family was waiting in Delhi, where an elaborate engagement ceremony would take place on the lawns of the Imperial Hotel in exactly a week.

"Iris is a complete airhead. She's self-centred and has never worked a day since leaving university. As for helping people, she's never even done a charity walk, as far as I know." He stopped, realizing how bitter he sounded. Kiku carefully rearranged the silverware on her side of the table, looking down all the while.

"Maybe she really is helping this family… if Iris can help find this missing child, the problem is…?" Kiku broke off, smoothing the tassels of the cushion.

"I doubt it. It's some misguided notion of hers that she can change the world."

"What exactly are you bothered about? Your parents and relatives waiting for you both to show up in Delhi for some big fat Indian engagement? You could still get there in time."

"No. I mean I care about that family stuff, but not like *that*. I've been wondering about our relationship, this wedding…"

The waiter interrupted the conversation with a tall glass of cold coffee and a murky *kalboishakhi*. Danesh took a sip of the drink and grimaced. Kiku thanked the waiter politely. She leaned in conspiratorially, almost touching his hand. "You should go to the Shambalasisa tomorrow. It's just a little hill where the Buddha preached the fire sermon but it's all about freeing yourself."

"Huh?"

"You know, freeing yourself from desires. The desire for control… over life, over others, over things that are not meant to be under control."

"This is not about control. Or about desires."

"No?"

Danesh looked into her eyes while she held his gaze. "Maybe some of us like our desires and don't want to misplace them on fiery hills?"

Kiku clinked her glass to his. "Cheers to that, but there is more than one kind of desire. If you don't know that already, you will be downing many more… of those!"

As she looked at his murky glass, Danesh could feel his father inside his head, filling his thoughts with a lifetime of lessons on what a real Punjabi man should be. He had grown up in a home where the man of the house swept dinner off the table if the salt was inadequate in a dish; his father terrorized them all with absolute control. It had taken him many years of watching other families to realize that this wasn't the norm.

His mother had taken Danesh's quick temper calmly – 'Boys will be boys, you can't expect them to sit quietly in a corner, their bangles louder than their mouths.' Kiku had spotlighted that dark recess in his mind: that urge to seize control, especially when Iris was around. When his first wife had so inexplicably left him, he had quickly latched on to a fiancée who needed him *more*. It hadn't mattered whether he had really loved Iris or not. He saw this, for the first time, absolutely clearly. No one else had forced him to question his feelings for Iris. Certainly not Iris. They had moved seamlessly into becoming a couple and the

167

great sex had made it easy for him to think that Iris was the right one. Now, sitting in front of Kiku, he was sure he had made a mistake. He loved talking to this woman, and spending time with her in these dusty streets had been an adventure. Although it was scary having someone get into his head so easily, he felt both liberated and aroused, as if the layers had fallen off one by one and he now stood in front of her, utterly naked.

*

The first *kalboishakhi* was followed by another and the drinks then stretched to dinner. He realized that he had been drinking all evening, which could also account for this surge in his sense of well-being. He looked at Kiku and decided that he had finally met a woman who was, in every sense of the word, incandescent. Kiku finished munching on the *galouti* kebab in her mouth (very 'tip-top first-class special' as the waiter had assured) and said, "I haven't asked you what you do for a living."

Danesh's attention had been mildly distracted by the couple at the next table, who were in the middle of an argument. Or rather, the Indian man seemed to be pleading his case with growing desperation and the red-haired woman just looked disbelieving. Must be a pick-up, decided Danesh. "I make documentaries."

Her fork stopped at her mouth. "Really? I thought you would be a corporate type."

"No way. Do I look that boring?" Kiku's laugh rang out and the couple at the next table looked at them grumpily. "No, sorry, I think I'm guilty of stereotyping. Asian-Americans are still fairly rare in the creative fields."

"You're right. I thought my dad was going to do an Uncle Sen when he found out I was changing majors in college…"

"An Uncle Sen?"

"Iris' father, Uncle Sen. He had a stroke when Iris moved in with a white guy who was also an art major in college… Iris had to move back home. Uncle Sen hates the 'arty-farties'. He barely tolerates my career."

Kiku looked down at her kebabs and speared one. "That's physiologically impossible – having a stroke on demand. Come on!"

"Well, you would think so, but it happened." He added softly, "Thankfully my parents didn't have a stroke when I flunked out of med school or got married then soon divorced."

There was the clink of cutlery as she digested that information followed by the birthday group whooping and whistling again. "So tell me about the documentaries you make… are you as famous as the Indian guy making horror movies… um, the '*I See Dead People*'? He was in some ad when I was in grad school in New York?" Kiku held her chin, thinking.

"Night Shyamalan? Yeah, he sorta made it OK for guys like me to make movies but my dad still thinks I'm such a loser for not making med school." He smiled wryly, "But he's glad I'm not a chef – now *that* would be terrifying!"

"And what do you want?"

"Oh, I love what I do! Right now I am working on this project called '*Borders/Crossings*', which will be a series of documentaries tracing the lives of people who have crossed borders. Globalisation, but interpreted loosely, so I've shot one on East European women who came as mail-order brides to the Midwest and another one on Filipina migrant workers in New York... that sort of thing."

The waiter began to clear their dishes. "Tea, coffee?" They both shook their heads and asked for the bill. A whoop went up from the birthday party again, causing Kiku to cover her ears.

"You'd think that the brats would have lost their voices by now," said Danesh.

"I think I'll lose my hearing first. This place is really noisy... listen, you want to come up and talk some more? I am supposed to leave Shambala tomorrow evening, so we may not get a chance to talk again. Unless you're tired, of course..."

Even if this were a completely platonic invitation, spending time with Kiku would beat sitting in his empty room waiting for Iris to call.

"Sure," beamed Danesh, "that'd be great." The waiter reappeared with the bill in its black leather folder, and Danesh reached out to take it. "I'll get this – I owe you one! I still can't believe how you went out of your way to help me find Iris – and find her we did."

Kiku widened her eyes. "Oh, come on! You'd have found her on your own... after shouting at everyone along the way!"

They stopped at the reception. No call from Iris. Danesh asked for phone calls to his room to be rerouted to Kiku's, then found himself on a couch in Kiku's room, with a steaming cup of green tea in his hands. It was refreshing after all that alcohol, especially as his right temple was starting to throb.

As Kiku powered up her laptop, he heard the first chords filtering out, faint and unclear. She clicked on the volume controls until the sound quality was a little better. "It's the latest release by a Dutch-Indonesian musician from Amsterdam and he's very good. You talked about crossing borders… I thought you might enjoy this."

"Dutch-Indonesian? This sounds too slow for my taste."

"He's quite flamboyant… just listen to it!"

Danesh sipped and listened as Kiku settled into the single armchair and sat back with her eyes closed. He realised that he really liked her eyes – they had a wide-eyed quality and he could imagine her as an anime character with a short skirt and incredibly long legs. She would probably throw him out if she knew exactly where his imagination was going.

"Like the music?" she asked after an interval.

"Don't know yet. Very gloomy."

Kiku still had her eyes closed. "There was a calligraphist painting some blood-splatters onto a large projection screen when he performed this at the Concertgebouw in Amsterdam. Quite an impact. The critics think he's a bit shallow though." She opened her eyes briefly. "And you?"

"I like it." Danesh wanted to hear Kiku's voice, but she quietened again as the Dutch side and the Indonesian side performed in different beats and keys. Danesh could hear the Asian ensemble in a minor key to a gentle beat, while the Dutch were represented by a full western orchestra playing a pounding rhythm. Then the music faded into the background as Kiku murmured about living in Leiden.

She had first met this Dutch-Indonesian man as her salsa partner, both of them going for dance lessons every Wednesday at the community centre. Leiden, through her sleepy words, came alive as a magical city, with dark green canals lined with black ducks with white-streaked beaks, gently bugling along in the late evening. She would turn a corner and there would be a poem, painted on the ancient brick wall, in its original language; a Dutch water lily poem rose out of boldly painted leaves and blood-red poppies burst through a Turkish poem. She had met dear old friends like that, unexpectedly, crossing over the bridge and finding Walcott, Pound and Neruda, even Rilke and Borges. One, day, walking past the Hortus Botanicus, it was Michizane who had greeted her with the Japanese lines:

> *If the east wind blows this way,*
> *Oh blossoms on the plum tree, Send your fragrance to me!*
> *Always be mindful of the Spring,*
> *Even though your master is no longer there!*

Danesh felt a mild irritation as he pictured a swarthy young man, Kiku's head tucked into his neck while they danced to a throbbing beat. He had been turning the CD case around idly, listening to her voice, the music rising and falling around them, as the cadence of her voice warmed him from within. He wanted to move next to her on the couch and take her into his arms now.

As Kiku fell silent, Danesh opened the case to read the insert, skimming over the lines, thinking about what to say to her. He thought that he had to say *something* – he didn't quite know what, but the thought of seeing her for only another day was unbearable. He felt the *kalboishakhis* coursing through his blood as liquid courage. But the phone rang, breaking the spell.

Kiku jumped up to reach for it. "Danesh. Yes, one minute." She stretched the cord so it would reach Danesh, then walked towards the bathroom, shutting the door with a click.

"Hello?" He could hear breathing on the other end, then Iris, uncharacteristically nervous. "I've been trying to call you for almost two hours, but the meeting just finished."

He looked at his watch. It was 11:45.

"Are you with… Kiku?"

"Yeah, we've been talking. How was the meeting?" He sounded abrupt, even to his own ears. He could visualize Iris lacing her hair through her fingers and pulling hard, as she did whenever this tension entered her voice.

"Lakshmy's a bitch, but we need someone like that who can stand up to them all. The way she talks as if I'm from another planet, really pisses me off… Dan? I was worried about you. Is everything OK?"

He tapped his foot on the carpet, three times. Then said, "I'm fine."

"Look, I'll try to be there as soon as I can, OK? Lakshmy's coming over to talk to the family and Laila and I need to be there, in case we're missing something important from the orphanage visit? Lakshmy says that if she doesn't find anything, she'll take me to the police commissioner, and I'll give a statement about how much I was quoted for Piya. It probably won't work with just my testimony, but we'll try anyway."

"OK."

"I'll see you as soon as I can, babe."

"OK."

"Look, it's really late tonight for me to come out and I'm tired and you sound bushed too. Tomorrow?"

"I said OK!"

There was a brief silence, then the sound of her indrawn breath. "Dan, they make babies just disappear overnight, we need to act fast."

"Right." He heard the water running in the bathroom over the silence.

"OK. I'll see you tomorrow then. Oh, and my parents just called."

"Your dad's calmed down now?"

She forced a light laugh. "Yeah, sorry Dad gave you such a hard time. Ma was quite apologetic. Dad's trying to make sure that money will be available in case I need it…"

"Great. Hope things work out with this baby thing."

Silence.

"Thanks. Take care, babe."

"You too. Bye." Kiku came out of the bathroom as he put the receiver down. She had scrubbed her face and broke into a gentle yawn that flared her nostrils without opening her mouth.

"I should go," he said.

"Yes," she added softly, "I'm quite tired."

The phone rang again shrilly, interrupting them. Danesh grabbed at the phone, thinking Iris was calling back. "Hello?" There was silence on the other line and the buzz of static. "Hello? Iris?"

"Who is it?" asked Kiku simultaneously. He could hear a sharp intake of breath and then the phone was disconnected.

"Wrong number," he told Kiku.

"Well good night then. Thanks for dinner," she said.

He could only say a soft "Good night" while she watched him leave.

Chapter 17

Lakshmy Mittal summoned Roop home. Roop made it very clear that Aman had not been forgiven; she would only return for good when her baby was returned to her arms, "Here," she said, hitting her bosom hard, "here is where my milk is drying up and feeding my fury."

Maitri stood outside, talking to with the group of teachers from the Buddhist School, until Lakshmy appeared with a stranger. He was tall, and definitely not Indian, although Iris could not make out his features as he stood outside the door in the dim light.

"This is Zoran Cavallero," Lakshmy introduced, "from Italy." She stepped in and looked at the expectant faces, "He's an international child rights activist and is helping me with the Chaya case." She headed for the charpoy, a little flustered.

"What a cool name, Zoran!" Iris said, and she held out her hand. Zoran bent his head and kissed the back of her hand.

"Ireees," he said, "Lakshmy has told me all about you."

Iris threw her head back. "Hmm? Really? I have been to your country once... we were on a cruise through Croatia and we boarded in Split, I think... then sailed all around Italy."

"Ah, yes. Split. You saw the Diocletian Palace?"

She nodded. "I loved the old city... especially the Agora at night."

"Then you must come back to Europe."

Lilavati cleared her throat and they both headed towards the charpoy. Zoran sat next to Lakshmy as Iris sank to the floor, cross-legged. She was getting very good at this; even squatting on the Indian-style toilet was easier now.

As Lakshmy opened her file, a long red card fell at Iris' feet. The cover showed a golden palanquin with a veiled bride peeking out, while a colourful butterfly hovered over her head.

"What's this?" asked Iris, picking it up. Some of the gold glitter came off the picture and winked on her fingertips.

Lakshmy grimaced. "It's a card from an abortion clinic in Orissa."

"A wedding invitation?" Lilavati peered at it from a distance.

"Hah, that's what it looks like! Open it... It says 'Pay Rs 2500 now to avoid Rs 250,000 in future.' Because an abortion costs much less than a daughter's dowry. Not very subtle, but very effective as a marketing tool."

"That's disgusting!" said Iris, quickly handing the card back.

Lakshmy shrugged, "I've seen worse." She addressed Zoran, "I'm going to speak in Hindi, so just try to follow along."

Zoran gave Iris an exaggerated eye-roll as the waves of unintelligible words washed over them both. Iris tried to catch the gist of it, but Lakshmy spoke too fast.

Aman, she suspected, spoke a dialect that she had no hope of understanding. It was clear that Lakshmy was practiced in this line of interrogation. She asked questions, reframing them in different ways, and looked at the whole family for answers in turn. Then Laila, sitting with her younger sister close by her side, stood up. She held herself upright, as if pulled up by an invisible string from her crown, and addressed Lakshmy very formally, as if delivering a presentation in front of an audience.

Iris knew her well enough by now to catch the excitement in her voice, but she could also hear the respect for Lakshmy. Before Laila could finish, Roop stood up and slapped her daughter across the face. "*Chee!*" she shouted, and the rest was unintelligible. Commotion broke out. Aman and Lilavati were both talking at the same time as Lilavati shielded Laila, who had started to cry. Lakshmy said something sharply to Roop, then the lawyer sank on her knees in front of Laila and stroked her tearful face. Laila's younger sister started howling in sympathy.

"What the hell did she say?" Zoran asked no one in particular. Lakshmy kissed Laila on her forehead. "This child just said that the younger guard at the orphanage, the teenager, may have some evidence for us. He has a cellphone and is always taking videos with it." She indicated the children, "their school is very close to Anath

Aashray, so Laila sees him often. Apparently, he asks the girls to take off their clothes and let him take pictures. He pays. He harasses the girls on their way to school… sounds like jailbait."

Zoran shook his head slowly. "And this child is what, six years old?"

"Eight." Lakshmy drew in a long breath, "Anyway, this will work to our advantage. This teenager has his videos professionally copied. A video of a girl in Laila's school was used to blackmail the married man involved. If the guard has any evidence of Aman entering the orphanage with the baby or leaving her there, he may not have destroyed it yet."

"But isn't it a major holiday today?" Zoran asked. "How are you going to get the police to do anything on a holiday?"

Lilavati answered. "One of our neighbours is very friendly with the older guard. I was asking around about the orphanage. He can find out where the teenage guard lives and we will find him today."

Lakshmy already had her files in hand and was heading for the door as Zoran swiftly followed behind. Maitri grabbed Iris's hand to pull her to her feet.

Lakshmy said, "Everyone, just hurry! Zoran, see if you can get someone from the Central Adoption Resource Agency or anyone from Child Welfare Services on the phone now. I am calling the Minister for Women and Child Development – she owes me a favour. Maitri, gather with the teachers – we may need the presence of a large group."

Chapter 18

The call came in to Lakshmy at 3:45 in the morning: A dark blue van without number plates had stopped at the gates of Anath Aashray, and as the gates opened, more than one person could be seen milling about the entrance. The rain was incessant, the informer explained, making visibility very poor under the dim streetlight. Lakshmy was still trying to get some police forces deployed.

In the meantime, a small force of Buddhist schoolteachers stood guard, ready to form a human barricade if the van attempted to leave with any cargo. It was four in the morning by the time Maitri reached the orphanage, just in time to see the police storming Anath Aashray. It was raining heavily by then, and mud splattered the waiting women as the police cars drove through the gate and swarmed in. There was the sound of banging car doors, then a voice on a megaphone sounded a warning. Maitri heard a gunshot, then another, and screams from inside. She tried to make out what was happening, but the rain made it impossible to see anything clearly. She felt a twinge of fear for the orphans – if the criminals were armed, the tiny police force mustered at such short notice may be overwhelmed and the children butchered as hostages.

The teachers had been told to keep out of the orphanage unless specifically called in by the police. More gunshots rang out. The screaming grew louder, supplemented by the hiccupping cries of small children in distress. Lights were turned on all over the building. A small figure running into the garden from the side door was wrestled into the mud by a policeman.

Maitri checked that the small knife at her waist was still there. It was small, but better than nothing. She could only hope for the best. Finally, the policemen started coming out, pulling five handcuffed men and three women in their wake. Maitri stepped forward and counted twelve children walking to the police jeeps in a miserable huddle. Not a single baby was found in the building.

*

The teenage guard from Anath Aashray was spending the night watching a pornographic video featuring failed Bollywood starlets. The grainy quality of the much-duplicated video left the images unclear but the soundtrack made up for it. When the police kicked down the door of the shuttered video store and ripped the poster of the latest blockbuster movie (the one which had cost fifty-one crores to make) into three jagged pieces, the teenage guard thought it a routine piracy bust, which meant it wasn't his problem. This store was filled with wall-to-wall pirated copies of every kind of movie available in the world, and he was, after all, a client. But old instincts died hard, so he tried to run as soon as he heard the first thump of police boots on the metal shutters. Unfortunately, the small viewing booth was so tightly wedged with sluggish men in various stages of arousal that a quick getaway was impossible. He sustained a black eye in the ensuing scramble (the boxed DVD collection of the Telegu softporn series *Thunder Thighs Throbbing* hit him squarely in the face as it tumbled from the highest shelf), and still reeling from that pain, he was amazed to see the motley audience being dismissed with a few slaps around the face or an indifferent whack with the baton, whereas he, of all people, received more than a few slaps from two burly police constables who pushed his face down on the concrete floor and handcuffed him very roughly. This totally shook him up. It didn't help that through his good eye he could see a little girl from the school near the orphanage – had he filmed her at some time? And she was pointing straight at him.

He decided to make life easier for himself. He was, after all, sixteen years old. Being beaten up by constables who approached thug-bashing as a form of entertainment made him wet his pants. His head filled with the images of the anal sex he had so delighted in taping. Horrified at the possibility of a similar form of abuse from the police, he had quickly confessed. Blubbering, he owned up to all the crimes he had ever committed, before he even knew what crime he was going to be charged with. It was only after he received a few thwacks for wasting the tax-payer's time that he understood this was about the totally innocuous footage of a baby being left outside the orphanage. Why did they want to know more about the old man who left a baby outside the orphanage and then returned with the rude rioters the next day? He would never understand the police. He looked at his bleeding cheek mirrored in the grimy glass of the police truck and concluded that his luck, indubitably, had run out. No wonder. The old women at the gates of the orphanage had been such a mass of black-tongued banshees that they had surely cursed Saturn into lumbering over into his astrological house of luck.

*

The day the baby had been left at Anath Aashray, the guard told the police, Aman had been able to enter and leave unchallenged. This was because the older guard was romancing the new maid from Chattisgarh behind one of the thicker hedges. The younger guard, knowing that such trysts usually yielded rich footage, had also abandoned his post to take some pictures. If the girl was young and sexy, the video would sell very well. The girl wasn't young but she was *very* sexy, and the younger guard had become so heated by the action that he had to handle his own relief. It was then that Aman had sneaked in and deposited the baby. Then the baby started to immediately bawl.

The younger guard, hearing the sudden ruckus, had automatically hidden. But he trained his camera towards the face of Aman who was now leaving, with the baby's bawling face clear in the background. He had quite a few seconds of this footage, as Aman had looked nervously back at the baby once then swivelled his head to check for other people, then looked directly at the camera again before leaving. The younger guard's phone was not only the sleekest model in the market, it could also shoot amazing pictures. The autofocus was sophisticated – with a digital zoom feature that made action sequences almost as clear as still photographs – and that alone had been worth the exorbitant price for this device. He could store about an hour of video before he had to empty the Micro SD card so he had plenty of time and he had let the footage roll.

The older guard, furious at the interruption, had jolted upright from an uncharacteristically acrobatic stance. Then he had hopped into his dusty pants, stomped to the source of the noise, having correctly assumed that the baby's wails would have attracted the Madam's attention. Unfortunately, Madam was already standing over the crib and had picked up the baby. She looked the guard up and down disdainfully and asked him whether he thought he was paid to roll in the dust like a two-year-old. Then she took the baby in.

All of this was captured on his phone's video. The younger guard had then switched off the video and whistled his way back to the guardhouse, looking as if he had just been away for a short toilet break. Had the older guard asked him where he had been or how Aman had managed to get in, the younger guard would have immediately showed him that lust-in-the-dust sequence and sold the footage to him. That would have been the end of *that*. Instead, the older guard had looked dejected all day, wondering whether his little escapade was going to cost him his job (it was the second time he'd been caught at it after all). So the younger guard had not thought any more of the salacious video, so rudely interrupted, but still in his phone's picture gallery. In fact, he had almost forgotten about the existence of this video. He thought about editing the raunchy parts and deleting the rest, but a preservation instinct had stopped him from doing so when the Madam had come to them late in the evening and given them a hundred-rupee tip each.

She told them to keep up the good work; every time a beggar approached with a baby, it would be best if they just disappeared from the guardhouse. Preferably not to roll in the dust on her time, she reminded the older guard slyly. The older guard had folded his hands and said, "You are my God," and he had bent deeply in gratitude.

The younger guard watched this exchange in silence, while his highly-honed survival instinct meshed into gear. He suspected that what the Madam was really telling him was that this video of the baby-drop may be valuable. A lot more valuable than the one hundred rupee tip that she had doled out so uncharacteristically.

He did not know why the police were interested in this video either, but he certainly could identify everyone on it.

Yes, he told the constables, the Madam and the other guard, of course, whomever they wanted identified he would do so. He would be happy to identify the maid from Chattisgarh as well, especially as her face didn't feature very much. No? Of course he could identify the man who had left the baby – he had his face clearly and in close-up too.

Chapter 19

Iris' mother, Nupur Sen could not believe that her husband, Dhiman, was promising to send $35,000 US to their daughter for some transaction involving a baby.

"Yes, you can have it by wire transfer, as soon as you need it," she heard him say on the phone. That was thirty-five *thousand* dollars, as in how much money some people made by slogging their butt off for an entire year. Had he gone mad?

They were seated in the office of the Himalayan retreat, in the one and only room which was equipped with a telephone. It was past midnight and the resort was asleep, but Dhiman, once he had established contact with Iris, insisted on calling his daughter back at least once every hour. This retreat was so deliberately isolated that only a Volvo bus peddling the route once a week could reach it. The disconnection from their real lives, which had seemed so attractive when they had bought the two-week package of detoxification of the mind and body, now seemed unbearably idiotic.

Dhiman harassed the resort staff with both bribes and threats, asking for a car, a helicopter, anything, anything to get them to the nearest city quickly, but the earliest any vehicle could be available would be in two days.

It seemed that Danesh had tracked Iris down, and now, there was some lost-baby problem Iris wanted her father involved in. Nupur had heard the details very briefly: yes, Iris was fine; no she wasn't with Danesh; yes, she really was involved in some scheme to rescue a kidnapped baby...

Nupur listened in bewilderment. The phone had no speakers so she had to piece together fragments from what Dhiman was saying.

"Iris is all right? Why don't you saying something?" Nupur asked when the phone call was over.

Dhiman sighed, "She is OK. But for some reason, she is still with that bookseller, and Danesh is at his hotel. I don't understand why Danesh isn't with her, helping with this missing baby..."

"It's just like Iris to cause some drama the moment we try and get away to relax for a few weeks."

"It seems the people she is staying with need her help. Or they say they do."

"Danesh has been running around all day. He must be exhausted. *You* should apologise to *him* for everything you said earlier today."

"Nonsense! If I were Danesh's age, I'd be right by Iris' side helping her sort out this baby crisis. Not resting back at the hotel. Hah, I bet he is hitting the bottle again, that useless fellow! That Mehra and his Son of Punjab, all just bloody Punjabi drunkards with no culture. He's 'tired'? What bloody nonsense!"

"If he's so useless, why do you want him married to our daughter?"

"Let's not start on that again, Nupur. The engagement party is only days away."

Nupur glanced at the clock miserably. "When are we going to Shambala? Is the car coming the day after tomorrow? Or you want to wait for the bus?"

"Of course we are going by car! I will help Iris find that baby. If that useless Danesh won't stand by her, I will show him that my daughter will never be alone in the world as long as I am alive…"

Outside, a bolt of lightning lit up the room. A storm had been brewing for the past hour, and before Dhiman had a chance to say any more, the lights went out. There was a moment of absolute silence as motors stilled everywhere, then Dhiman broke the quiet: "Ooof! This bloody pathetic country, why doesn't anything ever get any better?? How hard is it to get the power grid working reliably? Bloody third world issues!"

Nupur walked towards the open window at the other end of the office, intending to close it before the rain started. She felt the biting wind on her cheeks as in the dim light she watched the strong winds lashing the trees, which reached out to each other, the conifers and the shrubbery, all shivering leaves in a dance of solidarity against the elements. The wind was so loud that Dhiman's voice became a mutter in the background. And meanwhile, the mountains in the distance were being slowly dusted with a cloud of white, like someone sprinkling powdered sugar on chocolate.

As soon as the lights came back on, Dhiman was on the phone speaking with his personal banker in Ohio. Nupur sipped on the cold green tea left in a flask in the office. When Dhiman hung up the phone, Nupur picked it up.

"It's very late," said Dhiman. "You want to call Iris once more before you sleep?"

"No, I'm calling Danesh. Iris should be with him by now... but I have a bad feeling about this. I don't think we know the whole story."

Dhiman moved towards the door reluctantly, leaving Nupur at the phone alone.

"That *gobet*, a black belt and all, cannot even look after one little girl!"

Nupur waited for the door to click shut before she dialled the hotel number and asked for Danesh. She looked guiltily up at the clock again as the receptionist repeated the name to confirm it was the correct guest room. Then the phone's muffled burr sounded three times before Nupur heard the drunkenness in Danesh's hello. There was the hum of a music playing, and then an unknown woman's voice in the background.

Nupur had not heard this voice before; it definitely wasn't her daughter. Nupur stood there silently, unsure of what to do. She heard Danesh say, "Hello? Iris? Hello, I can't hear you," and then wait for an answer. Nupur heard herself breathing into the phone before she let the receiver fall back into the cradle.

Who was Danesh with at this late hour, if not with Iris?

Chapter 20

Danesh was unable to sleep after leaving Kiku in her room. He called reception to order some cigarettes, guiltily embracing a habit that he had tried to give up many times. It didn't help that, at the corner of his room, lay Iris' matching suitcases. One large with the smaller stackable one on top, both with distinctive black and red stripes. He realised that he should have asked her whether she needed her clothes – surely she did – but if she wouldn't bother to come to him, he certainly wasn't going to behave like a coolie at her service.

He needed to get his mind off women. He powered up his laptop and clicked on the footage of his latest documentary. He peered at the black-and-white photo from sixty years ago; it was a picture of a Bengali woman, a poet, looking defiantly at the camera. She was standing on the grounds of the University of Chicago, her hair as dense as the ivy on the walls behind her. She had come to America to confront her Romanian lover, a professor of Theology. Danesh spliced the music from an instrumental track into smaller chunks to experiment with the fit.

Their love story was told in the two books the two writers had written; his salacious, hers more judicious, and the music needed the different moods. The Romanian scholar and the Bengali woman had fallen in love at a time when even inter-caste marriages were forbidden, but he was visiting Calcutta to learn Hindu theology under her father's tutelage and that was how the teenaged poet had met him.

Now, in the poetry of pixels, Danesh was attempting to tell their story. This story of doomed interracial love had captured the imagination of many in Europe and Asia, and a few years ago, the story had been made into a blockbuster Bollywood movie. The Hollywood version, with Hugh Grant, had unfortunately faded into obscurity.

Danesh turned the CD around to read the names of the composers. The music was clearly missing something, and Danesh felt a sense of growing frustration. As the cigarette burnt down to its stub and he walked to the window to light another one, the sky was darkening with rain clouds although it hadn't rained. There was an ominous stillness in the air and not a single leaf stirred. Most of the windows were dark, but Kiku's window, in the adjoining wing, was brightly lit. He hummed a bar from the music he had just heard in her room and with a growing sense of excitement realized that Kiku's composer-friend had clearly tapped into a sense of loss. The poignancy of that composition would fit into his documentary perfectly – why hadn't he thought of this earlier?

He jerked the curtains closed and walked back to his laptop. He turned over the black-and-white picture absentmindedly, debating whether to go back to Kiku now. The Bengali woman was remarkable, not only because of her large eyes but the intensity of those eyes, that seemed to still burn with an inner fire through time and faded ink. Kiku's eyes were like that, luminous with intelligence.

He could only imagine the racism that had allowed this woman to be torn from her lover so violently and irrevocably, but then he remembered that his own mother's hostility to his first wife had been based largely on the fact that she was a dark-skinned South Indian.

Danesh lit another cigarette. He could read the clear misery of the girl in the poetry of the woman she had become. This girl never forgot the trauma, not even after giving birth to children, but she had forgiven. She probably knew that she was better off not having married the Romanian jerk, the man who had first touched her on those magical evenings and then written about it. But still, it had been worth it, a love that consumed so completely. He thought about his feelings for Iris. Yes, he was fond of her but did he love her in that all-consuming way? His mind slipped back to Kiku.

That look in her eyes when she had handed over the phone call from Iris, and the way she had looked watching him leave. He needed her now more than he'd needed anyone, ever. He felt reckless as he jabbed at the elevator button to go down to the lobby and walk over to the next wing. The alley of shops was all shuttered and the silence felt uneasy. A single young man with slicked-back glossy hair manned the reception and he nodded a greeting.

Danesh walked briskly past the pile of newspapers headlining, "Light at the end of tunnel for Baby Chaya?"

He had to search for her room on the seventeenth floor; he had blindly followed her up a maze of identical doors earlier and left in a daze. The corridor ahead stretched into rows of similar rooms, remarkable in their cloned facades and he tried to remember a familiar picture, a turn in the corridor, before gathering the courage to knock on a door.

There was the sound of a slow shuffle, the chain engaging in its groove, and then Kiku stood before him, holding the door partially open. He could see her grim face in the slight opening. He was too nervous for a greeting. "I need the music I heard earlier today."

"What? Why do you—?"

Her voice was sleepy, but not annoyed. As if she had been expecting him to return. "What time is it now?"

"2:22." The silence lengthened. He listened fearfully for a brusque *it's too late*, so he quickly said, "I need to talk to you."

"Why?" her voice seemed to hold only genuine curiosity. Danesh wondered whether he had been misreading the signs. "I'm leaving tomorrow, you know that."

Danesh felt his heart grow heavy, "Yes."

He felt her hesitate before she answered. "OK." He was glad that he was going to see her again, even if it was only to say good bye again. Her departure was still hours away. She released the chain and opened the door, "I thought I would never see you again." She looked at him solemnly, "Why do you need the music?"

"For my film… it's perfect."

"I'll find the CD… just give me a moment," and she started to turn away. He wouldn't remember the exact sequence of events but he had shut the door and taken her into his arms and she had leaned on him, perhaps just for a minute, perhaps longer, but they had stood there, silently, until he had picked her up and started to kiss her on the way to the couch. She held his hand (hers trembled) while asking him whether he was sure about this. She told him he was the most handsome man she had ever met in her life, and she just knew – from the first meeting at the Station Master's office – and then she had suddenly grown quiet, leaving what was on both their minds unsaid.

Danesh stroked her hair, hating himself for enjoying the sensation of it so much, but lacing its silkiness around his fingers anyway. What she said did not make much sense but it didn't matter, both were skirting around the inevitable. He kissed her to quieten her, and felt the intense pleasure of still being together, of having another chance. They made love on the couch, coupled into the crevice as if burrowing into each other's skins. In a moment of deep silence afterwards, thunder and lightning pierced the sky outside.

Danesh sat up as Kiku walked to the window. The rain was misting down. Kiku was framed by the gaudy green light of a hoarding outside and he thought she was the most beautiful thing he had ever seen in his life. He bent his face to hers and kissed the lone dimple creasing her cheek. Then he wrapped his arms around her waist and twirled her in the darkness until they fell on each other again, slightly giddy.

Chapter 21

Iris had just finished giving her statement to the police when she saw Shabnam, looking totally bewildered and moist-eyed, being brought into police custody. A lawyer trailed behind her, whispering into a cellphone. Iris had been at the police station with Lilavati, Lakshmy, and Zoran, for the past hour. She had already given a long statement about her meeting with Shabnam and now she nudged Lakshmy, "That's Shabnam, the one who tried to sell Piya to me."

Lakshmy looked up. "Yes, I know her. Zoran, I hope we can make the charges stick this time."

Flashbulbs were popping outside, and there was the commotion of reporters jostling for attention. A white woman with red hair was being steered through the door by a policewoman.

"That's Emily," explained Lakshmy. "Unfortunately the media's just latched on to a patriotic angle to this case and are framing this as the bust of an international child-trafficking ring. Those media animals are baying for blood… any person even remotely connected to Piya's case will be interviewed and redhead over there is front page material. Your countrywoman, Iris."

"Not quite," corrected Zoran, "She's Canadian."

Iris looked at Emily with interest. Under normal circumstances, she would have sympathized with this westerner in India in a difficult situation. Then she noticed Emily clenching and unclenching her hands and avoiding all eye contact. Iris felt hostility surge through her blood. "This is the woman who tried to buy Piya? She should look a lot more sorry than mad!"

Zoran said grimly, "Iris, she could say the same about you. *You* tried to buy Piya too, eh? Sometimes there are more victims than villains in these cases."

The journalists surged into the police station, surrounding Lakshmy in a raucous ring. Lakshmy knew the drill: "No comment," she kept repeating, "the Minister for Women and Child Development is due to issue a press statement outside the police station in the morning. We, my organisation, we have no further information."

Iris felt blinded by the flash of lights on her face as the photographers turned on her. She shut her eyes and turned her face to the wall as Zoran stepped between her and the reporters, telling the mob to go away.

*

There was still no sign of Piya by four in the morning. The rain poured down heavily, clogging the drains and causing mud to run in viscous streams through the roads, forcing cars and pedestrian traffic into the same muddy slosh. But in the darkness, after the long dry spell that had crackled relentlessly for so long, the sodden earth smelt like deliverance.

Iris, Lilavati, Lakshmy and Zoran sat in Café Chai, the 24-hour coffee shop across the street from the police station. It was a cheery café, one in a chain of orange and brown outlets across India. Iris was reading while Zoran and Lakshmy were both on their smartphones. Lilavati had finished a terse conversation with Roop and now stared gloomily into the distance.

Iris looked through the brochure of Anath Aashray to kill time. The brochure was purely textual, without any pictures of children, although it did have a large colourful logo in front. The orphanage had two hundred children, of which one hundred and thirty-five were orphans and the rest were destitute, and eighteen teachers. Source of Income: Public Donations. She turned the brochure over to read the plea for donations; highlighted in underlined block letters was the request to donate generously as the annual expenditure for the education of one child was Rs 7500 only. She felt too exhausted for any mental gymnastics, so she took out her cellphone and keyed in the exchange rate: 7500 Rupees worked out to be about 170 dollars.

"We will never find the baby," Lilavati was thinking aloud. "She could be anywhere in the country by now. They might even kill her now that they know the police are looking… if she wasn't at the Anath Aashray or the

Wings of An Angel Home, they have probably buried her by now."

"Stop it, Lilavati! They have nowhere to hide. All the major roads and airports and train stations have been blocked." Lakshmy said. "Also, the Minister needs some positive publicity from this; the elections are very close. She will make sure this case is solved."

"It's so easy to hide a baby, especially in the lanes of Shambala," Lilavati wailed on as if Lakshmy hadn't spoken.

Zoran clicked his phone shut. "They have arrested an accomplice at a road checkpoint. He had three babies in the car and they are now in police custody."

Lakshmy started to smile, but Zoran remained grim, "One of the babies is in a very critical condition. They want us to wait... doctors are looking at the baby right now."

The shocked silence was punctured by Lilavati's wails. The young crowd in the café turned to stare at the source of the noise. Lakshmy hugged Lilavati tightly to her chest as Iris and Zoran looked on helplessly, "We can only hope for the best Lilavati! There were three babies in the car!"

They sat whispering in Hindi, Lakshmy rubbing Lilavati's back in concentric circles. Iris sat uneasily, digesting the news. Nothing in her life had prepared her for the depths of human cruelty and despair she had to face on this trip. She suddenly found herself longing for loaded supermarket aisles and the smooth tarred roads where her volcano red McLaren would eat up the miles past luxuriant cornfields. She longed for control and abundance and shelter. Danesh was right, she was a complete foreigner here, she shouldn't even be here. Why had she thought she could make a difference?

Iris put her face in her hands. Who was she kidding about life in Ohio? Her own history had been carved from the misery of a mother who had sacrificed too much; had Iris ever acknowledged the abundance of her mother's dreams?

Zoran held her hands in his while he looked into her eyes. "You know, things have a way of working out, Iris. I deal with the most heartbreaking situations, and it's never as bad as we think it will be."

"Please. I don't want to hear about your bad situations right now."

"Well, sometimes, it's not bad, it's just difficult," He looked at Lakshmy, who was still comforting Lilavati. "Let me tell you about what brought me from Italy to India? It's a very long story, so stop me if I ramble."

"OK. But I think I need a strong coffee." They walked to the counter and sat on the high bar-stools, waiting for their numbers to be called. Zoran spun an ashtray on its smooth edge and started,

"About fifteen years ago a young Italian couple started to visit India every year to meet a guru. For spiritual salvation, that sort of thing. They would stay for about a month and come to the same place in India every year. For fifteen years they used the same taxi driver to take them places in the month they stayed here. Last year, when this couple came to India, they were shocked to hear that their friend of fifteen years, the taxi driver, had died in a bad car accident. His widow was caring for their five children, but she was destitute."

"And they adopted the children?"

"Well, not so simple. For one thing, India has some pretty crazy laws that haven't changed since the Hindu Adoptions and Maintenance Act of 1956. Like twins or siblings of the same gender cannot be adopted domestically. But the Italian couple wanted only the youngest child, a girl."

"Hmm. And how did the girl feel about it?"

Zoran tapped the table with his index finger. "She's three years old. Of course she doesn't want to leave her mother and her family! But her mother has agreed to let the Italians take her back to Italy, where the girl would be educated and well cared for."

"And… you don't agree?"

"I have no doubt that the child would be financially better-off. But that doesn't bring happiness, does it?"

"I don't know Zoran. Maybe this little girl will make a better life for her siblings when she grows up… like my family's money could help us with Piya now…"

"Well, that worked really well, didn't it?"

Iris sighed. "Could I have done something differently? I have a feeling I messed up."

Zoran reached out to hold her hands. "You were amazing. Really brave. You can't solve everything by throwing money at a problem." His gaze searched her face.

She watched his slight stubble, glinting gold in the light. "OK, I get what you are saying about the Italian adoption: You can have everything materially, and still not feel loved."

Zoran flashed an impish smile, "We are still talking about the little girl now?"

"Who else?"

"What are you doing with your skills, Iris? I hope you will stay and help us, even after this is over."

"Me? I am on my way to Delhi to get engaged!"

He leaned nearer and drew his forefinger on her bare hand and smiled, "No ring on that finger yet!"

Something in his eyes made her withdraw her hands and clasp them in her lap. "I'm *not* like Lakshmy and Maitri, or even Lilavati… they are so intimidating… I can't do what they do,. I'm not brave enough."

"You are stronger than you think. We could do with people like you." Zoran straightened up as she looked away. "Have you been up to Shambalisisa yet?"

"No, what is it?"

"It's where the Buddha found Nirvana. Not far from here. Very… inspiring, also a challenging climb. Would you like to go?"

"Nirvana! Seriously? I'll ask Dan… we should all go once this is over."

"Ah, yes, I heard the fiancée is in town."

Iris smiled sheepishly, "For a while, yes."

"Tomorrow, then, we will all go. Introduce me to this lucky, lucky man. If the weather's fine, OK?"

"OK."

They watched more press vans arriving, lighting up the square with moving edges. Then a police car left, followed by a convoy of screaming sirens. The lights had followed and now the façade of the police station was dimly lit by a lone neon tube light. Café Chai's orange and chocolate interior had emptied of patrons as only the four of them now waited.

"You should go home now," Lilavati said glumly. "It's late and I can wait in the police station. Aman is bringing Roop now – my daughter has bad cramps and she should go to Dr Chipalkatti instead, but she wants to be here when the police bring in the three babies."

"My contact will call. Soon." Lakshmy said. They will have the babies here anytime now. Once the Child Welfare and medical people are done with the examinations, I have asked for Piya to be returned. If she goes to a foster home or an orphanage, that's it, you can count on running around for weeks before you get her back again."

The large plops on the roof grew to a fierce drumbeat that fogged up the windows, enclosing them in an opaque cocoon. Iris didn't realise she had fallen asleep until the ringing of a phone woke her up. She had her head on Lilavati's shoulder so that Lilavati was awkwardly angled.

"Sorry," she said.

Lilavati did not hear her. She was talking to Lakshmy, "Is the baby OK?"

Lakshmy picked up her handbag and signalled that they needed to go. Iris scrambled after them, running through the pelting rain until they were at the entrance to the police station. Lilavati ran in, the other three following closely. There were three babies in plastic bassinets; one had bandages. Lilavati tottered on the tips of her toes, then moved forward again. A young policewoman in a dust-coloured sari turned around to pick up one of the babies. Iris stopped and screwed her eyes shut, *I can't bear to see this, I just can't. Please-please-please let it be Piya. Please let her be found. Let her be OK.*

She opened her eyes as the room broke into sound – Lilavati was holding a baby and jabbering in Hindi as she made extravagant gestures skywards. Lakshmy was thanking everyone profusely and shaking hands all around. Lakshmy turned to Iris and Zoran. "They still need to do tests on all the babies, but Piya seems to be fine. We did it! Congratulations everyone, we did it!!"

Iris felt herself enveloped into a group hug by Zoran and Lakshmy. She felt as if she'd achieved something worthwhile and glad tears sprang from her eyes onto Zoran's shirt – she did nothing to wipe them away. But Lilavati was still shouting in Hindi.

Lakshmy broke away from them both and rushed to Lilavati.

"Is there a problem?" Iris asked Zoran.

"Sounds like the baby will not be released today. They need to do a thorough medical check-up, make sure that the babies are returned to the right families… it's a lot of work. They can't just hand back a baby like a borrowed book, no?"

Lakshmy led a resistant Lilavati away and signalled Iris to follow. "We'll get Piya back in tomorrow," Lakshmy assured Lilavati. "They have to close this case properly first. The police will be coming to ask everyone more questions. Don't worry Lilavati, I will be here, and the baby will be back with the family very soon…"

Lakshmy gestured to Zoran. "Go with the driver and drop Iris back at her hotel please… it's too late for her to be wandering around alone. The Minister's press conference will be happening soon, so call me from the car, we'll need to talk about that." She squeezed Iris's hand, "Thank you, beta. You have been so strong!"

Iris turned to look back at the three babies. There was nothing she could do but return to the hotel now. She saw Roop and Aman rushing in through the doorway as Zoran led her away.

Chapter 22

Vidyut felt euphoric. The two people facing him across the table at one of Shambala's palatial homes were – finally! – the Indian Brangelina. They wanted to adopt their first child and then adopt others so that they would have a child from every state in India. Depending on how Indian states were formed and reformed, and whether they counted the union territories or not, Vidyut could be dealing with thirty-five separate adoptions for this couple... and they had come to *him*... to *him*! He felt like dancing a victory jig on the table right now. To create the ultimate patriotic rainbow Indian family, they had chosen Vidyut Kapoor of LifeSavers... but he could only grin like an idiot. It was a very early breakfast meeting (the woman was here for a movie shoot on the Buddha's life and this was the set). The day could only get better after such a fabulous start.

The woman was in a dusky rose chiffon sari which highlighted her Kashmiri pink complexion. Last year, she had played a bit-role in a Hollywood action movie and was now being flooded with offers worldwide. Although she had twelve years of Bollywood under her belt, Vidyut could only imagine her in that sizzling item-number; she had set the standard for vampy sexiness for the whole decade. Even now, thinking about her long undulating torso and chest, while her face was covered by a gauzy veil which suggested more than it hid, made him cross his legs.

No wonder she didn't want to ruin that beautiful body by putting any babies inside. He shifted in his seat, trying to keep from rewinding that reel playing in his mind. Her husband (like all the Bollywood leading ladies she was still officially unmarried) was a balding producer who was most likely funded by the Mumbai underworld. Vidyut had seen him in various publications, and most of them painted him in an unflattering light. The Babe didn't need him to bankroll her movies anymore, but it hadn't hurt seven years ago, when she had churned out five super-flops one after another.

This mansion was like an open lotus with its magnificent marble petals alight in the rising sun. He felt pleasantly soporific in the cool elegance of this ancient building. Leaning back slightly, he scribbled on a notepad.

"So do we want a boy or a girl?"

"A boy," said the husband.

"A girl," said the woman quickly, then squealed, "Janooo!!"

"Just joking yaar! Anything you want, Janooo," and they exchanged air-kisses like in a censored love-scene from a 70s Hindi movie. It was quite nauseating, but Vidyut could only grin. He and LifeSavers were finally face-to-face with Bollywood Royalty, and, who knew, Bollywood today, Hollywood tomorrow… his skin goosebumped with the possibilities ahead.

The children would live like little princes and princesses! These people had four servants to look after her one poodle; the groomer, the walker, the massage therapist, the pet-food chef.

"Um, Mr Kumar…" she began. This was the third time Vidyut would be correcting her. Little people didn't count; she looked like someone who would call a succession of servants Ramu just to keep things simple.

"Kapoor," he said gently, "Vidyut Kapoor. Like Raj Kapoor, Shammi Kapoor, y' know?"

"Right." Did she just roll her eyes?

"I want a baby that is *perfect*, no complications at all, not like that slutty Ms World who adopted that lame baby for maximum news…"

"Physically-challenged," Vidyut suggested automatically, but she didn't seem to hear him.

"No problems, you understand? This adoption is not about putting a halo on my head, no no, no."

"She is famous enough already," added her husband.

"No tamasha of any kind. Like despo Ms World I will be a single ma, but I don't want to pose-shose in a too-large home with Janooo's photo everywhere."

"Most Indian women adopting girls *are* single," offered Vidyut brightly.

She looked at him as if that were the most irrelevant statement she had heard all week. Her husband frowned, as if concerned that his wife's classification under 'most

Indian women' was a slight. Vidyut smiled apologetically. He could kick himself – he was still a bit jittery from the news that Lakshmy Mittal was making calls and sniffing around again. He wanted Shabnam to confirm that it was just a minor issue, no big deal really, and all was well at her orphanage, but he had not heard from her all night.

He looked at his phone in silent mode from the corner of his eye, very discreetly, but there were no missed calls. He had a flight to Delhi in the evening to worry about.

"Just one little press release and then total privacy, please." The producer thought for a minute, "At least until the pretty baby can star in a major commercial with AB or SRK, that kind of thing."

Vidyut looked at them both, waiting for the sarcasm, but they both seemed to be in earnest about this. His phone vibrated; he saw Shabnam's name flashing. He smiled apologetically, "Excuse me, I *have* to take this," but the producer waved him away, as if they would rather be alone.

There was no greeting. "That motherfucker was picked up with a video of the baby and he's confessed to the police already." Vidyut found his heart pounding in his ears but he kept his voice low, "Who had a video? Of what?"

"Of the baby! Being dropped off by her father! My guard has a video and the *bhenchod* confessed to the police even before they beat the shit out of him. They have some evidence now and my contacts are not returning my calls."

"Calm down Shabnam, even Mittal can't hang this one on me," Vidyut said tersely. He disconnected the call as she began to shout. His lawyer was on speed-dial, but he hesitated. If Shabnam's contacts were not returning her calls, then it was time to call in the big guns. He had the number of the lawyer who had defended a gun smuggling ring quite successfully in Mumbai last month. He scrolled down desperately, trying to remember the lawyer's name. He could hear the woman trilling gaily from the other room, "Is everything OK Mr er, Kapil?"

*

When the police came to take him for what they termed some routine questioning, Vidyut was fully prepared. He was ready to take on the system. He had gotten rid of his celebrity clients and made some rapid phone calls then he had pocketed his American passport. His hot-shot lawyer from Mumbai was flying into Shambala now. Vidyut had to cancel his flight to Delhi, but felt he had the situation completely under his control.

After an hour at the police station, he wasn't feeling quite so confident anymore. He stared at the bare walls and reminded himself that he was an American citizen. A citizen of the United States. "They'll send aircraft carriers to the end of the earth to save you," he had been told by an envious still-illegal friend. When he had last contacted the US Consulate two days ago (before he had any idea that another baby was going to become a bigger problem) he was assured that they were doing all they could to help him with the Chaya case. They were, he was assured, absolutely, on his side.

He reminded himself that the woman who had made more than nine million dollars in adoption fees in Cambodia – she was reputed to have delivered a Cambodian baby to a Hollywood movie set in Africa – later served federal prison time only for visa fraud and money laundering. As a US citizen, it was possible to get away with buying babies around the world. Vidyut took a deep breath and fingered his American passport, which he had strategically placed in his shirt pocket, ready to be drawn like a weapon when required.

He certainly wasn't going to allow himself to be slapped around like the neighbourhood thugs he had seen lined up on his way in. The problem was the media was here in droves and talking in soundbites about prosecuting perpetrators to the fullest extent of the law.

Shabnam had said something about a video before he had hung up on her, but he had no idea what shit she was involved in. He wasn't even sure what crime he might be charged with. He felt his unease morph into real fear and fingered his passport again.

The two police officers walked back in, with steaming mugs. No one had offered him anything to drink in the past hour. The older detective was probably in her early fifties with a severe hairdo and blunt nails which Vidyut glimpsed every time she stabbed at specific lines in documents. Now, she shuffled her files and took out a piece of paper. "Here are the death certificates for baby Piya's parents. Have you seen them before?"

"No," said Vidyut. She extended another piece of paper, "Here's the birth certificate to show she was born three months ago. Have you seen this before?"

"No," repeated Vidyut. He had known of the existence of certificates like these, always processed to ensure that the three-month window to reclaim a child would never be available. But he really had not seen these before; Shabnam never shared more information than was absolutely necessary.

He stood up to hand the documents back, holding them on edge as if they were contaminated. "I have been telling you for the past hour that I have had nothing to do with forging documents. I am a citizen of the United States and LifeSavers is about saving lives... I want my lawyer present."

The cop, who looked like a mafia hitman in a policeman's uniform, sauntered over to Vidyut's side of the table. His mustachioed upper lip quivered as he forcibly pushed Vidyut back into his seat. He leaned over him menacingly, spitting a mist over his face, "Do sit down Mr Kapoor, and don't raise your voice." He spoke in a dialect of Hindi, exaggerating the polite form of address. Vidyut nervously fingered his passport again. The man twisted his lip, "You think your government is going to bail you out of this, don't you? Hah? If we manage to convict you, all your consulate pals and your World Bank brothers will deny ever knowing you." He blew smoke into Vidyut's face. "We see it happen all the time."

"I had nothing to do with buying this baby or forging her papers. Or anything else... You should ask the people who run the..." he pretended to think and mispronounced the name deliberately, "this... An-at Ash-ray... about this."

"Shabnam? I think she's confessing right now. The police interrogation is very effective. Once we get going, that is." The woman looked at the man and he stepped over to the other side of the table again.

"Mr Kapoor, we have a video of the child being left by her father at Anath Aashray," she checked her notes, "… three days ago. Did you know that the father and grandmother tried to get the child back?"

Vidyut put on a bewildered look "Shabnam did tell me that there was a disturbance outside the orphanage two days ago but it was nothing unusual. Was that linked to *Emily's* baby?"

The woman sighed softly, "You should know that according to Indian laws this document of surrender," she pushed another piece of paper towards him, "has to be attested by at least two other people. Did you make any attempt to determine whether these two people even exist?"

"No. Shabnam takes care of that."

"It's the responsibility of the social agency to which the child has been surrendered. You are the American counterpart of that agency… why did you not look into this?"

"These things have always been handled by the Indians. We are based in the US; we just don't have the resources to validate every Indian legal document." He felt on surer ground now, "My government has said that they cannot control or be held responsible for the lawlessness here. I am licensed in America, and I fully follow the laws of my country; I expect no less from my Indian colleagues."

The man rose and walked around the room slowly. He faced Vidyut again, "How interesting, Mr Kapoor! People like you are trying your best to make children an export item, like any other. Hahn? Isn't that it?."

"No! Not at all… LifeSavers is all about giving under-privileged children a better quality of life."

"If, out of those under-privileged children you mention, even one is taken from their natural parents against their will, that's one too many for us, Mr Kapoor. Healthy children, like the ones you deal with, are very rarely given up for adoption… like the child you call 'Emily's baby'. Where is this baby now?"

"How many times do I have to keep saying this… Shabnam has the baby and I was merely representing Emily in this adoption process. I had no idea that this baby was *not* an orphan… in fact, I was told the whole family died in a tragedy… some wedding party car crash. If you stop a legitimate organisation like mine, you will leave these children open to starvation… and prostitution."

The man held up a hand and spat out savagely at Vidyut, "The saddest thing about adoption is it allows animals like you to trade in our children and get rich and still feel good. That's how you feel, isn't it, as if you jumped into a crocodile-infested Ganga and plucked a few babies from the swirling current?" He stabbed at Vidyut's forehead with a force that slammed his head against the tiles, "Let me tell you it's only in your fucked-up mind, Hero."

"Enough," said the female detective. She pushed her chair back and stood up.

*

Emily looked up as a man and a woman exited from an interrogation room, the man slamming the door hard behind him.

"That motherfucker Kapoor!" He stuffed his fists deep into his pockets. "And this scumbag will go right home to America on a first class ticket once his lawyer gets here. I hate this job on days like this! Fucking moron!"

The female detective looked at her notes and grimaced. "I hear Agarwal's defending his case, which means he will probably get away with it. Let's see. He's the one linked to the Chaya case, did you know that? Did you see how he had his statistics lined up… 'India sends thirteen thousand children abroad for adoption annually… six hundred go to America… those six hundred children live much better than the eight thousand children who work at factories making matches or carpets…' blah blah. He could have gone on for hours just vomiting statistics."

"OK. I'm going to go outside and cool off for fifteen minutes. Then we do this again before Agarwal gets here. I'm not giving up."

The female detective smiled grimly. "The building is full of activists and the media. The Minister is waiting for some soundbites. Don't hit this guy; we need his help to figure out exactly what happened with this baby."

*

They had confiscated all electronic devices at the metal detectors at the entrance and Vidyut felt vulnerable not being able to call anyone. It had now been three hours in the police station and he sat alone on a wooden bench outside the interrogation room, waiting for them either to call him in or to tell him he could go home. This was a nightmare. It couldn't be happening to him. He found himself praying hard, *Please Ganesha, let this pass and I won't step into this sordid country for the next decade, I swear it.*

He planned his future feverishly. A friend had bought a shop lot in Columbus right next to a strip club with neon pink lights and had offered it to LifeSavers to rent. Vidyut had taken one look at the sleazy customers at that rundown strip mall, the gaudy neon sign of an undressed woman with pert breasts under the legend *MEOW!* and he had sneered. No parent would come here to find a child to adopt. He now calculated that it would be an excellent site for an all-you-can-eat late-night buffet. All the drunks staggering home from strip clubs and the various bars in the wee hours of the morning would find the best kebab rolls in town.

He looked at his watch and wondered if he would hear from Agarwal soon. How long did it take to fly to this hellhole from Mumbai? It had started to rain hard again: *piss from the skies too whydontcha?* He looked up to see Emily emerging from another room. She ran her fingers through her dishevelled hair and sat down next to him on the backless bench.

"How long have you been here?" she asked, as nonchalant as if meeting at a summer barbecue.

"Almost three hours now. You?"

"Two. I was here late last night as well, as soon as they found my details in Shabnam's files. For some reason they thought Piya was with me, after they didn't find her in any of the orphanages."

When Vidyut didn't react, Emily said, "They have been very polite, but it's almost noon… I want to go back to my hotel."

"Are they stopping you?"

"No. But they need to know what happened to the baby. Or babies… they found more than one."

"If I knew, I'd have told them by now. This is not something I am responsible for… LifeSavers *saves* babies, we don't make them disappear."

A policewoman came and offered Emily a ride back to the hotel, which she accepted. She turned to Vidyut, "Its good bye, Vee." She jerked her head back to indicate her interrogation room. "I think I just saved your sorry ass in there. This stinks, but I didn't catch you doing anything illegal, so I had to say so. But you'll hear from my lawyers."

"I didn't *do* anything illegal, so just cut the crap." He didn't have to put up with abuse from her too.

"I'd watch my tone, kiddo – I saw the news reports on your other baby case, but thought you were OK. So I was wrong," she shrugged self-deprecatingly, "My bad." She looked at him contemplatively, "Just to let you know, I'll be doing an exposé on international adoptions for my newspaper as soon as I get back to Toronto. And once I find out what's going on, you're not getting away with this."

Vidyut flashed his best genial used-car salesman grin at her. "Fuck off, kiddo. Go find your *Seven Syllables for Sweet* somewhere else."

*

Emily felt totally crushed. She felt as if a tornado had whipped through her life and left her in a dark cold place, completely alone and without anyone to lean on. She couldn't break this to her family yet. Everyone in her extended family was already so invested in this baby that they would be completely devastated.

All those months of waiting which had felt like years followed by the few days of euphoria that now felt like minutes. She couldn't do this again… would never ever let this happen again. She had seen the signs, the Indian colleague had shown her the truth and yet she had deluded herself into this mess. It was her fault. Completely her fault. She had ached so physically for a baby that she had convinced herself that nothing else would have made her happy. She felt physically ill from this blow, but she had to face the media.

She had been fielding questions from various journalists from the time she had been brought in for questioning. As soon as Emily emerged from the police station, the flash of press photographers exploded on her face as a stutter of flares. She grimaced and walked along quickly, the policewoman's fingers on her elbow. They passed a circle of people and a passageway opened to allow her into the centre. A woman (someone whispered in her ear that she was the Minister for Women and Child Development) stood with two attendants holding babies in their arms. The Minister spoke at length in Hindi, stopping to pose with the babies, lifting one up and then another, then cradling both before handing off the bundles to a waiting aide.

Just as Emily was beginning to wonder why she was even in this media circus, the Minister turned to Emily and said in English, "It is also our duty to ensure that innocent foreigners are not misled," she touched Emily's shoulder, "like our friend here who has come from Canada." She pronounced it Kun-eh-duh and Emily smiled nervously, causing more flashes to go off.

"My government will take this to the parliament next week and we will fight to modify the child adoption procedure for Indians as well as foreigners. We have already reviewed the existing guidelines and have included mechanisms to control the exploitation of adopted children by all unscrupulous people."

There was scattered applause and Emily understood, by the policewoman's gentle nudge, that it was time to leave. The Minister ceremoniously extended her hand for Emily to shake. Flashbulbs went off again. She could hear a journalist questioning what the new procedures would mean. The Minister smiled warmly, "As per our draft guidelines a procedure has to be followed for registration of all orphaned, abandoned and surrendered children. Adoption of such children will be done only after due registration."

"There is already so much red-tape in this and people are willing to pay to cut through that – how will more registration and paperwork help?" another journalist asked.

The Minister's smile did not falter as she changed the subject smoothly, "The state government is implementing schemes to uplift the social, educational and economic status of the girl child in every way possible…"

The flashbulbs all went off in her face as Emily burst into uncontrollable tears. This was all so fucking messed up. She had had enough. Emily could hear the Minister getting fainter in the background as the policewoman hustled her away and into a parked car. Some journalists were shouting questions at Emily even as she fell into the seat and the policewoman shut the door behind her.

She couldn't believe herself. Where was this weakness coming from? Even in that horrible year when she lost her job, was labelled incompetent as a journalist, and then found medically to be infertile, she had never broken down. Now her teary face would be in the newspapers. She would have to pull herself together, then call her parents and give them the bad news before they saw her on CNN or something.

She checked her watch; she would give herself another half hour to pull herself together and then call, yes, that would be the best. She was sobbing into wet palms now. So many years of planning, so much time and effort and money, such belief in this miracle, all gone. She had thought foreign adoptions were an easier option, and definitely safer – there would be no birth-mother changing her mind at the last minute – but she had landed in a cesspool of corruption instead. It could have been worse; she could have realised how rotten the system was after she had adopted the baby. But the baby would have been hers by then…

She remembered the warmth of the baby in her arms and felt a sharp pang in her body again. Then immediate fury at Vee, at a system which allowed children to be bought and sold so easily, at herself, for having known of LifeSavers' court cases in Andhra Pradesh and not believing that something like this could happen to her. Now that it had struck home, she wanted to write an article immediately. There is no fool bigger than one who wants to be fooled. But her outrage was trumped by her sense of loss. All she could do right now was remember the weight of Piya in her arms, and how right it had felt. Through the haze of her tears, as the rain-drenched streets of Shambala sped by the window, the face of Piya, framed by such beautiful dark hair, was the only image she could still see clearly.

Chapter 23

Kiku was there next to him, sitting on the edge of the bed. It was eleven in the morning when he opened his eyes and Danesh was half-afraid that it had all been a dream, but there she was, in one of those silky kimono-looking things that he wanted to pull right off her.

Her brow was furrowed, but she smiled as soon as he sat up, fully awake. He wanted to reach for her, but it didn't feel right. "When did you get up?"

"It's been a while. I need to go down and check on my parents." She hesitated, "We check out at noon today so I was about to wake you. I wanted to say good bye."

He kissed her on the lips, mouth closed. This relationship was too new to not worry about morning breath. "So, what's next?" he asked softly. She looked away. "You go back to your fiancée, and I go to Kalyangarh."

"No," he said, "I want more than that."

"I'll still respect you…" she tried to joke.

"Not funny," Danesh held her hands tight.

She readjusted herself on the bed, sitting cross-legged. "Look, last night got more – um, emotional than it should have – I didn't intend this to go so far. I don't sleep with every hot guy I see, OK? And you were going to your engagement for chrissakes… this is just too complicated! Let's forget this happened at all."

Danesh found himself getting angry, "So thanks for the memory? That's it?"

She smiled softly, "I have to leave today… I've changed my travel bookings, arranged for the interpreter, the musicians are all there… I can't let my whole research team down."

"I'll come with you." Danesh was surprised at the quickness of his decision. "Yes. I'm not supposed to fly back to the US until two weeks later anyway, so I would have spent the time in Delhi. This engagement… I can't go through with it! I'd much rather be with you."

"Don't be ridiculous. I'll be in India for ten more days before I go back to Holland. And then what?"

"We'll take it one day at a time." He kissed her fingers, "I don't want to let you go. I just can't. And I can't get married… just like that… not after last night."

"And Iris?"

"I'll talk to her. Today. Right now. It wasn't working out… Iris and I – I mean clearly I suspected this, but now I know for sure. I'll go to that book-seller's place and just tell her…"

Iris' stricken face flashed across his mind and he had to tamp down the guilt that washed over him. He realised that he had fallen into a relationship with Iris to make himself feel better after his wife left him. And to please his mother. Meeting Kiku had opened up the possibility of something more.

Kiku seemed to be thinking, then she flung her arms around his neck and kissed him hard. "OK, but this is just for amazing sex for ten days, don't get any long-term ideas."

"Good. Then we wash our hands of each other," Danesh grinned nervously.

She drew away. "My parents are leaving for Japan in a few hours. I'm not going to tell them anything about you." She looked at her watch, "They'll come up soon if I don't go down for lunch. Go!" She shoved at his shoulder lightly.

Danesh started to put on his clothes. "When will I see you again?"

"I'll drop them off at the airport and be back at about three to pick up my bags. My flight to Kolkata is at six in the evening…"

"Send me your details and I'll get on the same flight." She pushed him out gently and closed the door.

*

Danesh swiped the card-key on his door and walked in with a goofy grin, remembering how Kiku had tasted last night. He felt like jumping on the mattress and leaping into the air as if it were a trampoline, but he settled for taking a running dive into the bed.

He slammed into a body and was startled to hear a shriek. *Shit! Whose room was this?*

The blackout curtains were drawn, making the room very dark, despite the morning sun outside. Danesh leapt off the bed and stood at the side, quickly switching on the bedside light. Iris was as wide-eyed as him. She greeted him with a delighted yowl as his body became rigid with shock. "How did you get in?" He finally managed to ask.

"I told them I was your fiancée. They believed me because of my American accent – What's the matter, Dan? Aren't you glad to see me?"

"I'm surprised that they just let people in like that… of course, I'm glad to see you… but what dumb security." He realized he was babbling and forced himself to shut up.

"Actually, it's the guy with the seriously gelled hair; he knows you and he recognized my voice from the times I'd called reception. I *am* your fiancée, so it's not like he made a mistake."

Then Iris leapt out of bed and he realised that she only had some lingerie on; a very sexy two-piece that showed yards of skin through black mesh lace, with a huge red bow in front that barely held back her generous breasts. Two smaller red bows were tied at the hips. He felt his penis stir. *Uh-oh.* She twirled around like a ballerina, and fell on his lap.

"I feel so good, Dan! You know, we got the baby back, it seemed like mission impossible but we did it! We were at the police station until like *all night* and then I just wanted to come straight back…" She was chattering on, and he let her. She was so happy, so genuinely proud of her adventure ending so happily that he couldn't say anything. Not Just Yet.

She went over to hug him but he sat there, unresponsive. "What? What is it?" They had known each other for far too long. Or perhaps he still smelled of Kiku. She knew immediately that something had changed.

She put her arms down and gazed into his face. "Where were you anyway?" Then, after a small pause, she grew incredulous. "You were with someone else all night?"

He could only be brutal. "Yes."

She threaded her fingers together onto her mouth to stop her lips trembling, "I don't believe this is happening…"

"I didn't plan on this happening… but Kiku and me, we…"

She laughed a hollow little ha-ha that made him want to take her in his arms and soothe her the way he had so many times before, after a bad exam or a rotten day. He had felt responsible for her well-being for so long that he had to will his muscles not to move.

"Two… no…" she counted on her fingers, "Two and a half days ago… it was *you* and *me. Kiku and me?*"

"I'm sorry, Iris. I don't know how to even explain this… it just happened."

"It just happened? Am I supposed to understand this *just happened*? How long will this new relationship last, Dan? Until this woman also runs off somewhere too? Because you are so capable of sustaining a relationship, aren't you?"

The failure of his first marriage was his sore point and she knew that; he hadn't thought her capable of such a low blow… he finally reached out for her.

"Don't touch me!" she hissed. Then, more calmly, "I should just go now."

"Where?" She ignored his question, pulling on her clothes quickly, rumpling them badly and ruining her hair. He noticed that she was now wearing a new salwar-kameez that still had a white price tag on; it was one that he had not seen before. As she shoved the clothes that were strewn about the couch into her open suitcase, he realised she must have had a bath here, probably preparing herself for their reunion. She gathered the last pile into a ball and slammed the lock shut.

"You can stay here, Iris! Listen to me! I'll make the arrangements for you to go back to your folks, first." He paused, "I'll stay and make sure you're OK, before I go anywhere."

"Don't tell me what to do, Dan." She turned her face to him, "Get out of my life. Now! OK?"

"Where will you go?"

Her eyes glittered with tears. "I'll be fine."

He realised that he had been following her around the room, his arms dangling uselessly by his side. He stopped and held her shoulders. "I am *so* sorry."

Iris wiped away her tears. She looked down at the toes she was clenching and unclenching. "Go with her, Dan," she said softly, twisting her shawl around her hands, "just go. And if you ever feel like coming back to me, don't."

He took out his wallet and retrieved a wad of notes. "Here's some money, Iris. In case you –"

She strode to the door and held it open. "Keep your money, Dan. I can manage, perfectly."

*

Iris walked out of Hotel Shambala International pulling her two matching bags loaded one on top of the other and her handbag slung on a shoulder. She dragged the weight aimlessly along an uneven road until she reached a large shopping mall, where, under a flowing fountain, no one noticed her tears. Then she walked into the cyber café on the second floor. Facing a computer, she steadied her breath and began to write an email:

> *Dear Ma*
>
> *I can imagine how worried you and Dad must have been, so now that it's all over, I want to say, thanks Ma, for always being there for me.*
>
> *I think I hurt you by not calling you or Dad, but it was the first time in my life I feel like I did something important, by myself. I'm ok, really I am. I was with some nice people – they looked after me well and I learnt a lot. I met some amazing lawyers who fight for children's rights and some awesome women so it's been an eye-opening experience.*
>
> *Ok, here's the news I want to write because I don't want to talk about this (not yet, so don't try to call, I really mean this.). Ok, here goes: I broke up with Dan today. Danesh found someone new while he was looking for me. Her name's Kiku and she's Japanese. I haven't figured out what I'm going to do next. But I know that marrying Danesh would have been a mistake.*
>
> *I need a few days by myself now. Email if you want to, but please don't call or look for me.*
>
> *Love you, Ma.*

Iris read over the email and decided that counting to ten and deleting the email would be the best way to get this out of her system without upsetting other people.

One—two—three—
She hit *Send* and stared gloomily at the screen.

Chapter 24

The tiny yellow guesthouse was nestled in a lane near the large mall. Iris felt her heart lurch when she saw a red signboard advertising rooms available. Orange marigolds spilled from the window boxes. Overall, it was an impression of riotous yellow-orange-red colour. Iris' bags clattered over the raised edge of the entrance, but no one looked up. It was a busy place, full of foreign backpackers, and she decided to stay here until she figured out what to do next.

"Do you have a single room?" she asked the receptionist.

"How many days?"

"Just one. I may extend it." It felt like a privilege to have her handbag with her credit cards again. She'd never take access to money for granted in the same way again.

The receptionist handed her a key with a large wooden handle and pointed her towards the garden. Her room was in the corner, facing a tiny square of lawn where some people were gathered around someone playing a guitar. She nodded a greeting but walked quickly past them.

She felt her pocket sing with an incoming phone call. She still had Danesh's mobile and he was calling her, again. She felt too exhausted for any talk at all, and switched the phone to silent. Lying back on the bed in a tiny room and examining the popcorn ceiling, Iris wondered what to do next. If her parents had their way, she would be on the next flight back to Ohio.

Iris imagined the plane nosing its way up into the night sky as Shambala glittered below her, criss-crossed by overlapping highways running like molten gold, while stretches of isolated lights twinkled in the blackness. It was a city that never stopped moving and Iris had spent two sleepless nights here. She felt her stomach growl. The last thing she had was the coffee in the middle of the night and she couldn't remember when she last had a full meal. She felt her eyes closing, even as she worried about her parents tracking her down, just as Danesh had, and her life shifting back into its groove.

Her parents were probably on their way to Shambala right now and that email she had just sent would not make a bit of a difference. She would have to say her good byes soon. She burrowed her forehead into the cool cotton of the pillow, certain that she would never meet anyone quite like Lilavati or Maitri or Lakshmy again. A host of memories played through her mind: Aman's shocked face at the railway station; Lilavati's belligerence at their first meeting; Laila lacing her fingers through Iris' hand in the auto rickshaw outside the orphanage. She remembered how soft Piya had felt the first time she had held her. Even the bad memories did not seem so bad anymore.

Scrotum-scratcher had been terrifying until she had stood up to him. And that meeting with Shabnam at the orphanage, ah, that had been the most frightening thing she had ever done, but she had pulled it off. She had learned so much from Maitri and Lilavati and she knew that the experience had changed her.

She felt herself unravelling after being a part of something so much larger than herself. Now that the stress was over, she realised that she'd enjoyed fighting for justice for baby Piya. But left alone and unanchored, she felt adrift. Iris turned her face into the pillow and began to weep.

*

Iris had fallen into a deep sleep and was woken by a call from the mobile vibrating near her ear. It was Zoran and she quickly answered, hoping for news of Piya.

"It's a beautiful day! Shall we go?"

Iris looked groggily at her watch. *What did he want?* "What... Oh, Shambalasisa! I forgot..."

The silence lengthened as Zoran waited for her to speak again. Iris felt a sob building up in her throat.

"Iris? Are you all right?"

Zoran barely knew her and he could hear her grief? How much of a mess was she? Iris cleared her throat deliberately, "I'm OK. Really tired from last night. Any news of the baby coming home?"

"Not yet. They are still working on it. Iris…"

"Can I call you back, Zoran?"

"What happened to you, Iris? You don't sound right. I knew I should have dropped you at your room in the hotel last night but with your boyfriend there…"

There was no other way to say this. "I just broke up with Danesh."

She could hear him breathing, and hurried on. "I've checked out of Shambala International. I'm absolutely fine."

"I'll come over, now. Tell me where you are."

"Don't. I'm OK."

"I want to see you, Iris. Please. Tell me where you are. Please."

When Zoran arrived, he held her for a long time, without words. Iris had stiffened at first, then melted into him, his silent frame holding her delicately, as if she were both precious and fragile. She had wanted that hug to go on, but had deliberately disengaged.

Zoran asked softly, "Feel like trekking to Shambalasisa now? It may be good for you."

She shook her head. "A long trek uphill? Not today. Let's go for a walk though, get out of this stuffy place."

She appreciated that Zoran kept the conversation going about Piya, about Lakshmy's efforts to ensure Piya's return sometime today or tomorrow. It was all good news and made her forget Danesh for a while.

They stopped at the bookseller, with the daily headlines from various newspapers laid out on a long trestle table. Iris was drawn by the headline: "This Minister wants to be Prime Minister?" and there was a picture with the smiling

Minister cradling the two babies in her arms while the red-haired American stood rigidly by her side.

Underneath that large attention grabber, about two columns away, was a smaller picture of Lakshmy Mittal. Iris scanned the article, reading with growing horror as Zoran riffled through various papers. The paper insinuated that the scandal of the alleged child-trafficking rings was to garner political votes for a floundering party. LifeSavers, the foreign agency implicated in the case, had already been cleared of all wrong-doing in Andhra Pradesh. Therefore, this witch-hunt was a stunt to insult the common man's intelligence and waste precious tax-payer money.

"Unbelievable!" said Zoran. He was looking at another paper, which he handed to Iris. This paper had a gentler tone, arguing that the agencies implicated in the scandal were only guilty of the kind of corruption necessary to cut through the paperwork in a society where bribery was a way of life. The papers vacillated between screaming headlines about 'Political Checkmate before Elections' or 'Child Trafficking Ring Busted: American Detained for Further Questioning'. There were pictures of Shabnam weeping and Shabnam defiant in grainy newsprint, as well as a shocked Mr Vidyut Kapoor.

"Are they making Lakshmy the villain?"

"Oh, I wouldn't worry about that, Iris. She's been through worse with the Chaya case. Even the international media picked up some of that nastiness, but she shrugs it off."

The shop owner came out and looked at them, unsmiling. "You are buying a paper?" he asked. Iris shook her head and walked away. Zoran paid for a paper and trotted after her, gently guiding her with a light touch on her elbow.

*

They walked for an hour before turning into the temple. The rounded white roof soared above intricately worked terracotta friezes depicting the legends of the Gods. The temple and its surroundings were beautifully maintained, and Iris sank into an empty bench in the middle of the green lawn. Two mynah birds were hopping near a tree and she remembered a childhood rhyme: 'One for sorrow, two for joy…'

Zoran lay down on the grass, his long hair splayed like his limbs. The temple doors were opening; it was five in the evening. No bells pealed, but her last prayer had been granted against the odds, when so much could have gone wrong. Baby Piya had been found. She breathed out her heartfelt gratitude.

She looked at Zoran, sprawled at her feet, his eyes half open. He was listening to something and suddenly he sat up to look in the direction of the sound. "Look over there! That potter's work is amazing, can you see him? And he's doing it without a picture or a pattern!" He was gesturing at the shed where an artisan was fashioning the image of a goddess out of clay. He had already created a base of straw and was now gently moulding the clay to fashion a torso and hands. There was a hypnotic repetition about his hands as he moulded the earth into the shape of womanly limbs, stopping only to moisten his hand with more water.

And she saw herself, the daughter of Dr and Mrs Sen, like that clay figure under a potter's hand, moulded by her parents' desires and dreams. When she had been 'given' to Danesh by her father she hadn't questioned it but simply gone along. She had never even realized that Danesh had taken over a parental role, with his fingers always on the small of her back and his height dwarfing her so that she looked to him for direction. Had he ever loved her?

She felt her eyes water. "That's the Goddess Saraswati... she has a book in her hand, see?"

"Gorgeous! So many beautiful goddesses and yet..." he broke off, embarrassed.

"And yet, girls have no value here? You can say it."

"This is not only an Indian problem, Iris."

"I know that. When I was in college I had a boyfriend, Aaron. When I moved in with him my father was furious. He said, 'I've made enough money here to forget our roots, but I won't let my princess marry the first pallid frog that comes along.' And that was that, especially when my father had a stroke... so then I got engaged to Dan. I thought I loved him, but I did exactly what was expected of me, like a mindless cow, being transferred from one farm to another."

"You're seriously telling me that you fell in love with a white guy and your father had a stroke? What is this Iris, some kind of a warning?"

He was too close. His eyes were the colour of warm brandy on a winter night and she couldn't look away.

"Maybe it is."

He leant forward and kissed her gently. A misty rain started to fall before the heavens broke loose with stinging arrows that drenched them in seconds. Zoran grabbed her hand and they ran up the steps to the temple for shelter. Huddled closely together in a corner, they tried to angle away from the pillared expanse that let in the wind and rain.

He was holding her as if he was scared she'd fall apart. "You don't really know me, Zoran. You don't even know my real name."

"Your name isn't Iris?"

"No, it's Shinjhini."

"Well… I like it. I like everything about you."

Her phone vibrated in her pocket. It was Ma calling. Good. She stepped away from Zoran to catch her breath. But Ma had none of the usual greetings for her. "Iris, we are at the airport, the flight is boarding soon. Your father's having dinner at the lounge but I wanted to talk to you alone. Are you coming to Delhi or not?"

"I told you, Ma! The wedding's off. No engagement party. Danesh has gone."

"It's really over? What will I tell his mother?"

"Tell her I grew up. I moved on."

"You did what–?"

"You know what a temper he has, Ma. He'd have been impossible to live with."

"That may be true. But–"

"You know it wouldn't have worked…"

She heard her mother sigh. "OK. We'll talk. Come home. You can take some time off, like those gap year things. Go to graduate school if you want."

"I don't want to go to grad school… I want to stay here in India. And work with this group that helps unwanted girls…"

"What rubbish, Iris, you will do no such thing. Your father will never pay for this.

"Ma, you know why I had to find this baby? I remembered what you had told me in Ohio when I was seven, just before you left for India. Remember? About Daddy losing you? About you losing yourself in a new country because you had no choices?"

"I did it all for you, you selfish girl – and this is how you repay me?"

"Ma, *you* showed me how hard it was to live a life scripted by other people." Iris paused, feeling her mother's fury in the silence. "And we are still too scared to change."

She could hear the shock in her mother's voice, "What's happened to you Iris? I don't know what nonsense you are talking about! I think you have gone mad. Yes, it's the shock of Danesh… Come back to Delhi, and you will feel all right again. Such ridiculous things you are saying… *Chee!*"

"Ma, what does Shinjhini mean? It's the tinkling sound of anklets, isn't it? I haven't heard my own name for a long time."

"*What* are you saying now?"

The line went dead in Iris' hand. She tried redialling but her mother's phone was switched off.

Zoran was at the other end of the temple. He had his back to her, and was talking animatedly on the phone.

"Iris!" He held her elbows and did a funny little jig, "Good news!! Piya is coming home any time, we have to go right now!"

Chapter 25

It would be a long journey. There was a strike in Shambala, one of those notorious *bandhs* which made public transport disappear from the streets and they were far away from Aman's district. They had to travel there in the back of an open truck. Iris negotiated the transport arrangements as her Hindi was fast improving; she realized that she was developing an eye for finding someone who could help, whereas Zoran looked so visually foreign that he was treated very differently. When men leered at her, she did not expect Zoran to put an arm around her shoulders protectively, as Danesh had done; instead she glared at the men until they looked away.

Zoran's hair streamed behind him in the open wind of the truck. Without a helmet or a seat belt, he looked as if he were flying. He had stood up, hemmed in by the tight pack of bodies crammed into such a small space and was shouting above the noise of the wind and the engine,

"Can you even imagine being able to do this anywhere else in the world? I *love* this!"

She had to pull him down when she saw a large pothole ahead. He had fallen next to her, still laughing. The roads were not smoothly paved with tar but lined with bricks and gravel and snaking speed breakers that jostled them together.

"This is it," said Iris in wonder.

"What?"

"*This* is the kind of journey I was looking for when I wanted to take that train ride. A crowded, jostling happy group of travellers."

Zoran took out his phone. "You want me to take a picture of you now?"

She shook her head. "No, sit down! I just want to enjoy it!" The ghost of Danesh flitted through her mind. Was he also thinking of her as often as she thought of him?

At the next stop, the breeze wafted heavy with the incense of *shefali* flowers blooming by the roadside. Dressed in ochre robes and strumming the *ektara*, a young Baul boarded the truck and began to sing the earthy lyrics of a song. A young college student sitting next to them confidently translated it for Zoran:

> *Sab loke koye, Lalan ki jat sangsharey?*
> *Everyone asks, what is Lalon's caste?*
> *Lalon says, my eyes cannot see the signs of caste.*
> *Look, some wear garlands, some rosaries around their necks,*
> *But does it make a difference, brother? Tell me,*
> *What mark do you carry when you are born,*
> *Or when you die?*

The song finished and Zoran started asking the singer a number of rapid-fire questions, which the college-student had problems interpreting as quickly. Money was exchanged, then the Baul's voice rose in another song.

"These guys are paid with rice and lentils, maybe sometimes a coin. Isn't it amazing, the beauty of what they create and how little they expect in return?" Zoran whispered.

Iris nodded. She felt so alive. She imagined spending her life wrapped in music and poetry, rediscovering a lost language, lost sounds, becoming relentless in getting her own way, leading a life of some meaning. Making a difference.

Zoran was listening to the song with his eyes closed. It was too early, she would have to make that clear to him. She was not interested in a relationship.

With his eyes still tightly closed, Zoran turned his face up to the slightly damp wind. It was an electric moment, the sky charged with dark clouds, so Iris too lifted her face to the heavens, letting the rain wash over her.

*

Maitri sat unperturbed as she stirred sugar into two tea cups and merely listened. Zoran had gone to meet Lakshmy, and now it was just the two of them, waiting inside Maitri's room. "I should face my parents. But I'm not sure what I want to do – stay or go? Maybe I'll just make a mess of things and hurt a child I want to help…"

Maitri rolled her eyes. "The children are stronger than you think. Start off by paying Aman for his broken stall... and just take one step at a time. If you take on the problems of the world, you will only face disappointment."

"Are you making fun of me?"

Maitri's cellphone rang again – Piya was coming home, she wasn't coming home... it was all rather confusing. Roop had gone back to her cousin's home and was refusing to come home unless the baby was there. Lilavati and the girls were also at the cousin's home. That left a bereft Aman wandering like an untethered bull; Iris could see his dark figure pacing outside.

Maitri was preoccupied but hospitable. "Stay for dinner," she invited Iris. "I don't know why you are staying at that guesthouse all by yourself! Are you hoping your man will come back tonight?"

There was a morose silence, before Iris said, "No, he won't come back. But he's like a habit I need to break. Don't you sometimes get scared, or lonely, all by yourself?"

Maitri put her phone away and looked at Iris. "Scared of what? My neighbours are here, my family of Buddhist teachers... this whole city is my family!"

"That's true, but you know, don't you miss a man?"

"You will stop missing yours!" Her voice grew serious. "My mother was a prostitute, Iris, I told you that, I think? I grew up in a brothel. When I was eleven, a customer too drunk to know the difference, mistook me for my mother while she was out, or maybe he knew, it didn't matter. At sixteen, I had a son who lived for eight days, and when they put him on my breast for the last time, I felt his tiny body getting colder. Nothing killed me."

Maitri looked away. "We survive. I kept studying with the nuns, no matter what happened to me, I studied."

"You never wanted to get married?"

Maitri chortled. "Oh a couple of times, a man here and there... some of them already married! But no one I wanted to chain my destiny to."

She indicated Aman, who was still pacing the common hallway outside. "Look at Roop – she will come back to this idiot fellow, maybe try again to have a son for him. Because no matter what he does on earth, unless he has a son to perform his funeral rites, he thinks he will go to hell. He'll go to hell anyway, but Roop will come back and make a life with him again, because every time she wants to register a daughter for school, or a thousand small things, her children will need a father in their lives. I have no children... no man either."

"I'm not so strong, Maitri. I can't imagine living alone."

"That's because you have no work. You don't need a man, you need a *laksh*..." Maitri struggled for the word, "A goal, to aim for? Like when Arjun hits the eye of the spinning fish..."

"Spinning fish?"

"It's a story in the *Mahabharata*..." The phone started to ring again, "Never mind, it's a long story about a hero who was not always a hero, but Draupadi, the woman with five husbands, loved him the most anyway."

Chapter 27

Firecrackers started popping at Lilavati's house later in the evening. Baby Piya was coming home! The house was alight with festivity. But Iris' own mood was sour; her mother had refused to speak to her again and her father sounded old and tired on the phone. She would go to Delhi as soon as she had said her good byes in Shambala; she owed her parents that. She had booked a seat on the last flight leaving for Delhi, and felt wretched. Through the open door, she could see Laila twirling like a dervish around the room, her arms spinning like windmills as her glass bracelets tinkled. Her shiny *ghagra-choli* glistened turquoise and pink with flashes of emerald green. Lilavati adjusted the pleats of her own sari as she smiled at her granddaughter indulgently.

Iris stepped into this happy scene with the e-ticket on her phone feeling like a ticking time bomb. She had plastered a fake happiness on her face, but before she could speak to Laila or Lilavati, there was the cacophony of a wedding band as Aman's group trumpeted a joyous march up the alley. The musicians were dancing with small children and women in an unabashed celebration. Men were singing loudly and beating on drums, while bringing up the rear.

As the musicians approached the house, Iris could see a line of saffron saris, headed by Maitri holding the baby aloft like a triumphant trophy. The neighbourhood children were dancing a jig around her and slowing her progress. No one seemed to be in a rush as they danced circles around each other. Beyond the sound of the trumpet and drums, in the tiny silences were the wails of a baby.

Iris felt her heart thrum with happiness as Roop flew out of the house as if on wings, followed by Aman and then Lilavati. Laila and her sister joined the dancers. There was a silence as Maitri handed over the swaddled baby and Roop cradled her in her arms. As Roop began to weep with joy and the raucous music and the frenzied dancing began again, Iris found herself weeping too.

Firecrackers went off in rapid succession, popping all around her. She saw Lakshmy and Zoran in the crowd as a blurry haze, still very far away. Laila ran to Iris and whirled in a merry dance. Iris caught her in mid-swirl, smiling at the grin stretching her face. "Your sister's back, Laila!"

Laila shook her head in a frenzied joyful dance, swirling amidst the riotous colours, her happiness so infectious that Iris started moving her hands too, in an improvised wild *bhangra* until she bumped into Lilavati.

"Ooof, there you are!" exclaimed Lilavati. "I was about to go get you! We wanted to call your husband also but I don't know his number. Call him now, invite him to come also. All the girls are in the house, Roop is back, so much to celebrate!" Lilavati bustled off without waiting for an answer, followed by a line of children. Two boys, dressed in clothes so stiffly-ironed that the starch lines cut cleanly through the fabric, were seated on a bed sheet folded lengthwise. In front of them was a *puja* plate, complete with a lit *diya*, whose flame flickered prettily.

There was a soft rustling as Roop and Aman appeared with Piya. "Thank you," said Roop softly. She was still crying. Aman had his hands folded in a *namaste*. Iris felt uncomfortable at such gratitude. Underneath her disquiet was the knowledge that she would have fled from this family a long time ago if she had the means to do so. Iris clasped Roop's hand but spoke to Aman.

"I'll pay you back… for the broken dolls, the shop. As soon as I get back to Delhi, I'll contact Maitri and transfer the money to you. Aman, I am so sorry!"

Aman, who held Piya in his arms gently pushed the hair away from the baby's face. He kissed the child's forehead and closed his eyes briefly. "Thank you," he held up his baby, "Thank you, Madam."

Lilavati bustled out of the kitchen, wiping damp hands on her sari. She glanced at Iris and then at the doorway, "You called your husband?"

Iris shook her head, unable to speak. Maitri exchanged a meaningful look with Lilavati, before putting an arm on Iris' shoulder and squeezing gently.

"Men!" said Lilavati contemptuously, "Did I tell you that I was married to a Pathan and a Christian? Good thing they died before they killed me!" She patted Iris' shoulder.

Her chuckle did not cheer Iris and she blurted out, "I'm leaving for Delhi soon. My flight is tonight and I can't stay long."

Lilavati's face softened. "You need to be with your family, yes?"

Zoran was incredulous: "You're leaving? So soon? Today?"

"I thought you were coming to work with me!" Lakshmy gave her a tight hug. "Come back! We could use your courage in this line of work." Iris stared at them both, her mind muddled by what Lakshmy had just said: *She, Iris, courageous?*

"Are you offering me a job here, with you?"

"Of course I am!" Lakshmy grinned at her, "We need good actresses in our line of work!"

"Thank you. That's awesome. But my mother isn't talking to me anymore... and there's stuff, in my own life, things I need to sort out first..."

Lakshmy looked puzzled, but Zoran understood immediately. "Just don't take too long and don't forget about us."

Laila was now at her grandmother's side and rubbing against Lilavati's arm with her body like a cheeky cat. Lilavati stroked her hair as they spoke in Hindi. Lilavati said something to Laila, then indicated the boys, "My cousin's grandsons. Roop has been staying with them." She sniffed angrily, "Now that Roop's back with that son of an owl, it's time for a little ritual."

Laila dragged her little sister down in front of the *puja* plate with a whoop. Roop sat down with the baby in front of the four children. The sisters both twirled the flame around the baby and placed a red mark on her forehead, then the boys did the same. Lilavati tied a red string around the baby's wrist. The two little girls suddenly burst into laughter. Laila held out her hand for something the older boy was not giving her, then she held him down and tickled him until he held out a silver package.

Maitri whispered into Iris's ears. "These are presents Lilavati bought for the children. To celebrate. Laila has been wanting this for a long time… watch her face."

Laila opened the package slowly, savouring the suspense, peeling away at the tape with the uneven edge of a nail. The silver foil fell away as something glinted inside. A pair of glass earrings shone like diamonds as Laila held them up against the light. Her mouth opened in delight as her sister clapped, jiggling up and down so that her own earrings danced happily too.

*

A table fan whirred noisily in the corner where Roop held Piya protectively in her arms; she had not let Piya out of her sight since getting her back. Aman sat by her side, stroking the baby's cheek. Roop leaned slightly against her husband's arm, letting him into the charmed circle again as she wiped away happy tears.

They had decided to keep her name – Piya – for she was indeed beloved. The family milled around her, still amazed at the miracle of her return. "I should go now," said Iris reluctantly.

Maitri smiled sadly, "I will miss you very much!" As Iris held Maitri in a long hug, she couldn't control her tears. There was so much being done by women like Lakshmy and Maitri and Lilavati. These women knew what they were doing in the world, and their hearts were so big. They had shown her what was possible, that she too, could change things for the better.

Iris sniffed miserably, "Thank you for rescuing me at the train station."

Laila sidled up to Iris and stood looking at her glumly. "I… English…" She stamped her foot and shouted something at her grandmother, causing Lilavati to laugh. "This child says when you come back, she will speak in English. She learns English at the school but no one speaks it and she is too shy to say anything now."

Iris reached for Laila's shoulder. "When I come next," she said slowly, "you will teach me Hindi."

Roop looked into Iris's sad face and offered the baby for a good bye kiss. Iris had cradled Piya in her arms before, but the miracle of the baby's softness and perfection took her breath away, just as it had the first time. Roop hovered over her anxiously until Iris handed the squirming baby back into her mother's arms.

Lilavati said softly, "We are poor people, but even with wealth, we would never be able to repay the debt we owe you."

"No no, I did nothing. Thank you for everything, for looking after me…" She tried to press some rupees into Lilavati's hands. "I owe you so much…" She looked around the room, unable to articulate such strong emotions. Lilavati gently wrapped her hand around Iris's hand in a fist, "Don't insult us, beta. It was our good fortune that you stayed with us. Keep your money."

Iris tried to remember the good bye etiquette her relatives used: "For the children then. Buy Laila and the girls something, some chocolates, sweets…"

Lilavati said firmly. "Come back and see us if you want to make the girls happy. I would insist that you stay longer but you should go back, to your home."

Iris felt gutted. She was going to miss this family, especially Lilavati and Laila. She had never felt as needed as this family had made her feel. Laila held out something wrapped in colourful tinsel, like that used to wrap toffees. She extended it towards Iris.

"For me?" Iris asked mischievously, expecting a chocolate éclair. She deliberately took her time in unfastening the two edges, unravelling what was inside. Laila's glass earrings now lay in her palm.

"I can't accept these," Iris said softly. "Laila, you love them, they were a gift for you…" she held them out in her open palm.

Laila's face fell. She looked down at the ground, and drew curlicues with her feet while muttering something.

"She says she wants you to have them, so you remember her," Lilavati said.

Iris bent down to hug Laila, but Laila squirmed out, unused to being embraced. Iris looked at the earrings in her palm again and remembered Laila twirling earlier, the glass earrings flashing; it was, without a doubt, the most precious gift she had ever received from anyone in her life.

Iris held Lilavati, in a long embrace. "Bengalis don't say good bye," said Lilavati tearfully, "Say '*Aashi*,' I'll be back."

"*Aa-aashi*," stuttered Iris miserably.

"*Esho*," said Lilavati softly. "Come back. Promise."

"I'll drop you at the guesthouse," said Zoran.

"Thanks Zoran, but I'll be fine. You stay here and enjoy the victory party."

"I'll walk you out then."

The whole family stood, along with a number of stragglers from the area, waving at her until she couldn't see them anymore. Iris was glad that just before she left she had tucked the money into Laila's schoolbag. Lilavati may have been too proud to take the money, but Laila, she was certain, would use it very well.

They were at the mouth of the alley when Zoran said, "You remember there is still a strike on, eh Iris?

'Yes, but I should be able to bribe my way to a private car... I know some drivers in this area now."

Zoran gestured towards a black fiat. "Lakshmy's driver, at your service. She asked me to make sure you reach the airport safely."

Iris giggled, "The Tigress is making sure the nuisance leaves?"

Zoran stopped and took her hand. He softly kissed the back of her hand, and she was reminded of the first time they met. Was it only two days ago? "We will miss you very much, you know that."

"I will miss you all too." Iris kept her tone light, "But I think I need to be alone for a while."

"I hope you find what you are looking for."

She touched his cheek with the tips of her fingers. "Thank you."

*

She had checked out of the guesthouse, her matching luggage was in the car and she was on her way. The car stopped at a red light. Tall office towers towered on the right, while on her left, genteel mansions reminiscent of leafy arbours and wide roads stood fortress-like behind guarded gates. Iris looked from left to right, considering the sharp contrasts in these two worlds.

Then she saw the little girl. Too young to be a traffic-light beggar, the girl tottered on legs that seemed so unsteady that surely she was just learning to walk? Her shapeless green dress was clearly sized for someone much larger and she stood in the thin partition between the two lines of traffic, one toe digging into the mud between the broken bricks. Only a narrow railing, painted in a garish yellow with peeling brown lines protected her from the manic traffic. The little girl briefly paused at a fluted rail before tottering on. This was clearly an accident waiting to happen.

The light changed to green. The traffic started to slowly move, the motorcycles screaming their impatience while zigzagging close to larger vehicles. The girl stopped again, picking up the edge of her dress to suck. Below her waist was a dirty brown thread, woven with a lighter string, a talisman of some sort. Below that, a swollen vagina rose unashamedly, the gape clearly labelling the girl's sex.

Iris shuddered as her car started to move. The girl was still tottering on this island between the traffic, poised for a certain death, yet the helmeted couple on a Pulsar ahead of her chatted on, shouting above the din and oblivious to anything else. The Skoda on her other side flashed its newness into Iris's eyes as she turned to look at the passenger, being driven by a liveried chauffeur, an iPhone glued to his ear.

Even if the girl hadn't lifted up her dress, Iris would have known. Only a girl would be so unwanted that not even another sibling would be sent to shadow her hesitant steps. Above the little girl's head was a municipal sign exhorting 'Keep Our City Green' and on top of that was the larger advertisement by an InfoTech firm: 'A World of Opportunities Awaits You'.

The little girl waited, staring at the traffic with interest. The three plastic bangles on her arm didn't glitter or jangle to demand attention. She flexed the toe that had been digging into the dirt and looked up. Her eyes met Iris' briefly before flitting away. Then the girl took a tottering step forward.

An auto rickshaw driver revved his engine, headed straight for the girl.

"Stop!" yelled Iris. "*Roko*," she added in Hindi for the driver. The Fiat slowed to a halt, raising a line of mud at the guttered edge of the road. The driver, convinced now that she was an eccentric foreigner, looked at her questioningly as Iris opened her door.

"Luggage?" he asked. "Bags?" He flicked the switch to pop open the boot.